# Sweet Georgia

## Unrequited Love Book 1

BreAnn Hanks

**Hanks Publishing**
Publish Co.

You can follow us, Hanks Publishing, on TikTok and Instagram!




ISBN 979-8-218-33848-0




Book cover designed by BreAnn Hanks

*Dedicated to cancer survivors.*
*You are amazing, beautiful, and talented.*

# Prologue

Georgia looked up at the statue, unsure of why she was here.

She was uncertain of a lot of things if she were to tell you the truth. Like how she got here! Did she get a cab? All she remembered was that she came from Alabama. She didn't know why she was so far from home in the first place!

Was she gone for very long? Was she on vacation? Why did she leave Utah?

Her mind reeled at the possibilities of why she left for Alabama. She remembered she always wanted to live there, get married, and have kids. Did she do all that? Should she go back? She shook her head. No. She wouldn't remember any of them if she did have a family! She needed to get her memory back, first. And it could start here in her home county. She just needed to find a way home first. She was flabbergasted as to how she got home in the first place!

She remembered grabbing the wallet on the counter of the house she was in. She didn't know why she was there alone. What on Earth had her memory been so fuzzy? She couldn't tell if she was in a dream or actually awake. Should she pinch herself?

"Georgia?" A female voice asked, thankfully sounding familiar.

She turned, recognizing the woman as if through a fog.

"Oh my gosh. Georgia!" Her best friend, Avery, wrapped her arms around Georgia's shoulders and slowly, she returned the hug. "You're home!"

"Yeah," she nodded, still feeling unsure.

"How are you?" Avery pulled back. "Are you hurt? Are you okay? He didn't do anything to you, did he?"

Georgia shrugged, confused as to who *"he"* was. "I don't know what you're talking about," she said softly.

Her best friend winced. "You have no memory of Alabama, do you?"

Georgia shook her head. All she could remember was leaving Alabama! Did she even have a life there? "Nothing."

Avery smiled sweetly. "Well, then let's go. You can tell me what you do remember in the car. Okay?"

Georgia agreed, grateful to have a ride with a familiar face that she somehow remembered. "Thank you, Avery."

"Of course," she breathed. "Who would I be if I didn't help my best friend out?"

It was Georgia's turn to smile sweetly. "Thank you."

"You're so welcome," Avery set her hand on Georgia's lower back and stood to her side, looking at her. "Do you remember Ashton?"

Blinking, Georgia looked at Avery in shock, her memory before Alabama seeming to be intact for some reason. Yes, she knew Ashton. Avery had been in love with him for years - "Nooo," she dragged out. "He didn't!"

Avery nodded her head and smiled brightly, holding up her left hand to reveal a big diamond ring. "Just last night!"

Georgia screamed, moving in to give her best friend a tight squeeze.

"I haven't told anyone because I wanted you to be the first," Avery explained. "You've always been like my sister, even if we don't have the same parents."

Georgia danced her feet excitedly. "I'm ecstatic! Thank you!"

# Chapter 1

## 6 Months Later

Georgia snorted and giggled, staring up at the bottom of the top bunk where her best friend laid. They were camping and sleeping in the toy hauler part of Georgia's dad's camper, and Avery had just told her an absurd idea about the scar on Georgia's stomach.

She'd discovered it this morning. She didn't know why she didn't see it before!

Laying on her back, Georgia kicked the bottom of the top bunk.

"Oh!" Avery went quiet as she remembered Georgia's dad and his girlfriend sleeping at the other end of the camper.

Georgia muffled her laugh and the cracks between the door lit up on the other side for just a moment. Avery peeked over the top bunk, her hand curling around the edge. Her blue eyes somehow glowed in the dark.

"I'm just saying," Avery started. "That scar could be from a kraken."

Georgia snorted in disbelief, looking up at her best friend with her hands on her stomach. "I'd have to see it to believe it." She said.

"Well, then let's prove it."

"Pffft! We're only twenty. Barely old enough to prove something so absurd."

Avery pointed down at Georgia, her arm extended and her eyes dancing. "You're wrong. We're more than old enough to prove anything!"

Georgia lightly smacked Avery's hand away. "I didn't get trapped in a kraken's mouth."

"Lair," Avery corrected Georgia. "That's how you got your scar."

"Like I can breathe underwater," Georgia shook her head in disbelief. "No. You're absurd."

"No. I'm reasonable," Avery said as Georgia rolled onto her side and fluffed her pillow.

"Insane!" Georgia looked up at her.

Avery put her hand to her chest, her eyes soft with starlight from the window. "I like to think of myself as an expert in mysteries."

Georgia plopped onto her backside, her brown eyes on Avery. "They're not mysteries if you're an expert."

"Whatever," Avery sighed. "I say you got your scar on your stomach from a kraken."

Georgia lifted an eyebrow, giving Avery a look that had been getting her to shut up since childhood. Sure enough, Avery put it to rest. She rolled onto her back, out of sight.

Georgia finally got comfortable, grabbing her pillow and snuggling into it. She started to drift off, but she woke when a truck pulled up next to the camper with its lights on. Blinking sleepily, she knew it must be her cousin coming up camping with his family. His trailer was already here.

"I still think it was a kraken," Avery said sleepily.

Georgia snorted for what seemed to be the tenth time and thrust her foot into the top bunk.

"Uh," Avery teased seductively.

"Heard that," Stephen, Georgia's dad, spoke up on the other side of the closed door between the toy hauler and the rest of the camper. He must've been in the bathroom.

"All in good fun, Doctor Rhinehart." Avery defended herself.

"Uh huh," Stephen dragged out, knowing full well what Avery meant by her seductive moan. He heard it way too often when Georgia and Avery were teenagers.

The two women would talk about a boy and whenever sex was mentioned by Avery, Georgia would smack her and get that sound from her. Avery had always wanted Georgia to lose her virginity like she did, but they couldn't both be nailed by the hottest guy in school. They certainly couldn't both marry him, and since Avery was now engaged to him, Georgia wasn't sure why she still bothered egging her on.

The bathroom light finally turned off and Stephen made his way to his bedroom, where his girlfriend was still sleeping. Georgia knew he had a good relationship with her, but sometimes she would catch him looking at Avery in a certain way.

Ever since Georgia's mom passed away from cancer seven years ago, Stephen had been attached to her and Avery more and more. Georgia knew that her dad loved her, but she couldn't help but wonder if he'd fallen in love with her best friend somewhere along the way.

There were twenty years between them, but still, as she drifted off, Georgia found herself worrying that he might make a move on Avery. This camping trip was her bridal shower after all, if he was going to do it, he was running out of time.

*~*~*

Stephen lay awake, unable to fall back to sleep.

Hearing his daughter with her best friend reminded him of the good old days and he missed them greatly. He wanted his wife back. He wanted his old life back! All the sweets that Rayleigh would make for their neighbors. All the times Stephen would sneak a treat whenever she wasn't looking! The times they danced in the kitchen or in their bedroom. And all the memories they had together growing up, having a life together, and having a family.

Don't get him wrong, Stephen loved his girlfriend. But…

He looked at Marissa as she slept. She wasn't Rayleigh. Or Avery.

Gosh, Avery… She was so beautiful and she had been there for Georgia and Stephen every single day. It was no wonder he got attached to her. Maybe he should tell her. Before the shower in a couple of days. Avery should know how Stephen felt about her. How in love he was with her. She may be his daughter's best friend, but she's also his. And as much as he loved Marissa… He loved Avery more.

Stephen sighed and sagged, wishing that he could sleep. But with Avery so close he couldn't manage it without her in his arms. He remembered the times she slept over and had a nightmare. Stephen would get woken up by little Avery and she would ask him if he would hold her like her father would whenever she had a bad dream. She hadn't done that since she became a teenager. But Stephen still remembered those times.

He wanted them back… The old times… Was that so much to ask?

Stephen looked out the window and the sky started to turn a lighter blue after what seemed like hours. Maybe it was just minutes. Stephen had been up all night!

Suddenly, Avery yelled out in her sleep, calling for Ashton a small thud following as though someone had fallen.

Knowing that tone, Stephen got up to help with her nightmare. When he made it to the door and put his hand on the knob, he heard his daughter talking to Avery, who seemed to be crying. Stephen's heart strings were pulled at the sound and all he wanted to do was pull Avery into a hug.

"That can't be right," Georgia said lowly. "He loves you!"

"I'm telling you, Georgia," Avery mumbled. "I saw him with Marissa yesterday."

"Isn't he, her son?" Georgia asked. "I mean… They look alike!"

"No," Avery explained. "He's not. Marissa's his aunt."

Knowing what the two girls were talking about Stephen opened the door towards him and peered around the door. His brown eyes landed on Avery's wet blue eyes. He wanted so badly to wipe her tears away.

"I'm sorry to interrupt," he muttered. "But I couldn't help but overhear. Marissa is Ashton's aunt. Whatever you saw, there was nothing but family love. I can promise you that."

"Thank you, Stephen," Avery breathed, her voice oh so soft. "But I thought I saw them kiss. On the lips."

Stephen winced, but he still gave Avery a side smile. "Common misconception with the family, Ave," he whispered breathlessly, watching the woman he so loved cry and break his heart. He wanted to wrap her in his arms and soothe her. But he knew he couldn't. "Marissa and her family are super close. You know that."

Avery nodded her head, trying to grab the concept of the closeness she had witnessed with the family multiple times. "Then I don't know if I can marry into it," she whispered.

"Avery," Georgia snapped softly. Her hand flew to her best friend's lap. "Are you sure? You've loved Ashton since the day he set eyes on you!"

Avery looked at Georgia and sniffed. "Maybe you're right. I should give it a day. Before I make a final decision."

Stephen sighed and leaned into the doorway. "If you need anything," he said gruffly. "I'm here."

Avery looked up at him and their eyes met. He could tell in her gaze that she was second-guessing her engagement to a wonderful man.

Ashton was such a good guy and always had been. He was considered the hottest guy in school not just because of his looks, but also because of the way he treated everyone. Even the geeks and nerds that would normally get mistreated by a jock like him. Ashton treated everyone as equals. He was truly a beautiful soul and Stephen couldn't say that about a lot of people he knew. Avery deserved Ashton.

But so did Georgia. Jake was a mistake. Stephen should never have let Georgia leave home with a twenty-year-old when she was just fifteen! He should've argued with her more! Won the fight! But at least she kept in touch with Avery…until the day she forgot everything.

Stephen nodded his head at Avery and looked at his daughter. Their twin brown eyes met and a message was sent between them. Georgia knew. And she wanted her dad to make the move if he loved Avery enough. If he didn't, he needed to let her go and never let her know. Stephen dipped his chin and gave his daughter and her best friend some time alone.

# Chapter 2

Georgia looked over at her cousin, Trevor, who'd arrived late last night. His trailer was already here, and she'd watched him put the slide-out into place before she'd fallen asleep. But she hadn't slept well, tossing and turning most of the night.

Avery made her think about her scar, making her wonder what actually happened. But could she think of any explanation? Not one bit. All it had done was make her more confused about what had happened.

Now, Avery sat next to Georgia, her hand around her drink as she shook with energy. They hadn't eaten breakfast yet and all Avery had in her system was an energy drink. She was going to be bouncing around soon if she didn't get something decent to eat. Maybe Georgia should help cook?

"Let's go for a walk," Avery put in.

Georgia glanced at her, finding Avery's blue eyes wide and wild.

"Tip some roaming cows or something."

Georgia smiled at her jittery friend. "You need food in your system. Then you won't be so hyper."

"Hyper? I'm not hyper."

"Excited, then."

Avery snorted. Her gaze moved away and Georgia followed her eyes.

Marissa was walking out of the trailer with her phone in hand. She looked ready to take a phone call. As a very successful business woman, she'd barely found time to come up for a night. She'd be leaving soon - she had to get back to California to close a deal.

Oh, Georgia hoped she found a man out there who didn't have his heart reserved for someone else.

Georgia had seen the love in her dad's eyes just this morning, when he'd come to help with Avery's nightmare. It wasn't fair to any of them, and she didn't feel any ill-will towards Marissa. She was an amazing woman, and Georgia had only ever wanted the best for her.

Trevor cussed under his breath as Stephen followed Marissa to her car. Did he drop a piece of bacon? Avery nudged Georgia's arm before getting up and walking over to Marissa. Georgia knew this was a conversation she had to stay out of, along with her father. But she still inched closer on her camp chair so she could eavesdrop. Besides, Stephen was going to be right there! Why couldn't Georgia?

"Hey, Marissa," Avery called softly, sounding truly sincere.

Marissa turned towards her.

"I'm so sorry you couldn't stay."

"Me too," Marissa nodded. "My business is always needing me."

"Speaking of business. I wanna start one myself. Where do you suggest I start?" Avery grabbed Marissa's wrist, a common sincere move that she pulled when Avery felt it necessary to gain someone's trust.

"Well," Marissa looked at the contact then looked into Avery's eyes. A soft, genuine twinkle lights up Marissa's eyes and she smiled sweetly. "Depends on what you wanna do."

"I wanna own a clothes store with jewelry I make myself," Avery explained. "I'm a designer."

"In that case, start out small," Marissa said. "Try a small online store and market on social media. Post something every business day. You'll also want to register your business right away and make sure you come up with a unique store name. You don't want anyone trying to steal anything from you. You want your ee, I, en number ASAP."

"Thank you, Marissa," Avery said.

Marissa tilted her head to the side, truly looking worried. "Are you okay? I heard you call out my nephew's name this morning. You didn't have a nightmare, did you?"

Avery nodded her head in confirmation. "Rough night."

Marissa trailed her hand down Avery's arm then gave her hand a squeeze. "Then don't marry him." She said softly.

Avery winced, her blond hair pulled back in a braid and bouncing off her back. "Excuse me?"

"We love you, Avery," Marissa sighed. "But if kissing my nephew is what it takes to get you to not marry him, I'm going to continue to do it."

Avery stuttered, unable to find her words. "But, Marissa-!"

The older woman got in Avery's face, her grip on her hand tightening. "Do you really love him?" She challenged Avery.

Avery snapped her hand out of Marissa's like she's been bitten. "Of course!"

"Then why do I always catch you with that boy that works at the grocery store?" Marissa asked. She didn't sound thrilled.

"Because he's my brother!" Avery snapped, angry that Marissa would ever bring her autistic brother into such a conversation. Why did she anyway? "Can I not see him?"

Marissa got stuck on one word, her eyes betraying her guilt. "Oh," she whispered, looking down. She took a step back, truly looking dumbfounded and stupid. "I am…"

"Marissa," Stephen started, sounding upset. "What were you thinking?"

Marissa looked up at Stephen. "I wasn't. When I saw Avery at the grocery store kissing her brother's cheek, I thought she was cheating on Ashton."

"They look alike!" Stephen grumbled, defending Shad and Avery. "He can't get a blue-collar job like most can!"

"I didn't know," Marissa said. "I truly thought he was Avery's secret boyfriend."

Stephen shook his head. "No. And if you're going to jump to conclusions like that every time, I'm ending it with you. Don't come back after you close the deal."

"But Stephen." Marissa tried to defend herself and Georgia pressed her lips together to keep herself from snorting.

She shouldn't be finding this funny. Marissa truly was an outstanding person with amazing qualities. And she deserved the benefit of the doubt. But Georgia should've known Marissa would've had the flaw of jumping to conclusions. Maybe she was only capable of thinking things through properly when it came to her business.

"We're done," Stephen growled threateningly. He stepped around Marissa, leaving her by her car with the door wide open.

Marissa turned around, watching him and trying to call him back. But he didn't listen. Instead, his eyes met Georgia's and she instantly looked down. He grabbed his double person chair and slammed it down, grabbing his daughter's attention. She looked up at him and she knew she was in trouble. He motioned at his chair with his head, his threatening eyes on her.

"Here or inside," Stephen said. It was a threatening question.

Georgia blinked a few times, knowing what her father was indicating. He could be easy on her or hard on her. She didn't know what was worse. Out here he would torture her with his disciplinary, disappointed glare. But inside… He would blow up on her and ask her what she was thinking.

She knew this had to do with her eavesdropping. It always did. Making up her mind, Georgia got up and started for the camp trailer. Stephen followed her, the sound of his footsteps making her hurry inside. Once inside he slammed the door behind him and Georgia sat down on the couch. The marble table was next to her while she sat on the comfortable leather couch, resting her arm on the top of the cushioned seat between her and the table.

"How many times have I told you, Georgia May," Stephen said roughly. "Don't eavesdrop on somebody that doesn't deserve it!"

"It's my best friend, Dad." Georgia looked up at him, wondering why he was lashing out. What had him so irritated? She shrunk back into her seat, knowing not to look away from the dangerous man. He wouldn't hurt her. No, he truly loved his daughter. Still, Georgia knew what he could do if she crossed him. "I was just keeping an eye on her."

His glare snapped at her as he unwrapped the bandages on his hand. Maybe the bite was what had him so worked up. He'd gotten bitten by a patient, a little dog that had lashed out in fear. Mostly healed, the bite marks on his hand were still there as a reminder of his mistake. Georgia knew, almost more than anything, her dad hated mistakes. And eavesdropping was never okay.

Stephen was ex-military. He'd been a doctor in the army, but retired early when Georgia was twelve years old. That had been the year her mom was diagnosed with ovarian cancer, and he'd made the choice to come home for them both. Now, he was a veterinarian. She knew he loved his job, but Georgia wondered if he ever missed being in the special forces. He never showed signs, but she still wanted to ask someday.

"Dad," Georgia whispered, trying to dampen his temper. "Please."

"Then don't make it so obvious, Georgie!" Stephen spat, making his daughter jump at his tone.

She stuttered, trying to find her words. She was scared, dumbfounded.

"When you eavesdrop, you make it obvious and that's when you get into trouble!" Stephen pointed at her angrily. "One of these days it won't be me that catches you! And I can't afford to lose you!"

Why was he so angry? What was *really* bothering him?

"Dad, I…"

"You're all I got, Georgia!" He went on. "I'm doing this for your own good!"

Georgia stood up, facing her beloved dad. "Then let me make mistakes."

Stephen slammed his hand on the counter, making Georgia jump. "No!"

"Dad!" Georgia yelled. "I need to make mistakes to learn!"

Stephen leaned forward. "You've already done that, Georgie! With Jacob!"

Georgia winced.

There was that name, again! Who was this guy?! Did he have to do with Georgia's scar? Did he hurt her? If so, she was grateful she couldn't remember. And maybe… Just maybe. She didn't want to have her memory back for that reason.

"For the last time," Georgia insisted, daring a step closer and take on her father. "I don't know who that is!"

"He's-!" Stephen cut himself off and looked down, his hand on the kitchen counter near the sink. He shook his head. "Never mind," he whispered, sounding defeated.

"No!" Georgia yelled. "I gotta know who this Jacob slash Jake guy is because it's all you and Avery talk about! You talk about him as if he was a bad guy!"

"Because he is!" Stephen looked Georgia straight in the eyes. "Georgia. He took you away from me." Tears filled his eyes, showing an emotion he rarely showed.

Georgia shook her head, not believing him. What could ever make her want to leave? Stephen was the best dad anyone could ever ask for! He may not have been there all the time, but he's made up for that!

"That's not possible," Georgia growled. "I would never," she took a step towards the father she always loved, "leave you. You need me just as much as I need you!"

"Then. Stop. Eavesdropping."

"*Dad*!"

"Georgia, Avery can fend for herself!" Stephen shifted and leaned into his hand. He winced, but he ignored whatever pain he felt. "She doesn't need you right there all the time!"

"We're best friends!"

"And she's my-!" Stephen cut himself off again and Georgia knew where he was about to go with this conversation.

Georgia had to confess to her dad. Before he or Avery got hurt. "You're her best friend, too," she mumbled. "I just wish the two of you would stop pretending. You deserve each other."

"Georgia," Stephen drew out warningly as Georgia started for the door.

She didn't listen and stalked out, where Trevor was practically making out with his wife. They weren't newlyweds, but they were so tangled up with each other that they didn't care as Georgia came back outside. Avery at least looked up at Georgia as she stalked past and headed for the four-wheeler.

Thankfully, her best friend didn't try to follow. She needed air. Time to herself.

Her dad wouldn't confess his love to Avery and she was going to marry the wrong guy! And if Georgia couldn't bring them together, then what or who could?!

She quickly swung onto the four-wheeled machine and started it. She backed it up, before putting it in drive and racing onto the dirt road, never minding the dirt that she left behind. She better not be followed by anyone!

# Chapter 3

Jake wrung out the towel over the bathroom sink and wiped off the excess of his shaving cream. He didn't like his scruff turning into a beard or mustache. He didn't know how some men could like having a full beard. He set his towel down as he heard the front door open and a truck speed by outside. Jake walked out of the bathroom and just about collided with his best friend.

"Here, let me kiss you," Bain teased. He wrapped his arm around Jake's shoulder and thrust him into his chest. Bain's lips met Jake's cheek, nothing new since he's usually like this when you collide with him.

Jake wrapped his arms around Bain, making the moment a little more intimate between them as they teased each other. Even though Georgia wasn't here to see it, Jake knew she would enjoy the funny moment. He acted like he needed Bain, clinging onto him teasingly. When Bain finally had enough, they let go of each other and green eyes met blue eyes.

"What's the verdict?" Jake asked, heading toward the kitchen.

Bain followed. "She's back home."

"I figured that much." Jake pulled a beer from the fridge and popped the top off with the tables edge.

Bain made a face. "She doesn't remember a thing, Jake."

Jake kept his beer in front of his chest as he turned to look at Bain in disbelief. "What?"

"Georgia. She… Doesn't remember a thing about Alabama," Bain explained. "Or you. My friend in Utah told me that whenever Stephen or Avery would mention you… She would get confused."

"That's impossible." Jake set his beer down on the table, forgetting about his thirst for a cold one.

"Doctors said it could last a while," Bain shrugged. "I mean… She got hit by a car!"

"And she miraculously lived," Jake said. "I know. I was there."

"Jake… She needs to come home."

"Don't you think I know that?" Jake snapped, glaring at his best friend.

"No. I mean…," Bain struggled for the right words. "She needs her memory back."

"And how do you suppose I do that?" Jake started around the table, but stopped to grab his beer, looking at it on the table. "Go get her and make her remember?" He looked up at his best friend, not wanting to go to Utah. It's the last place he wants to be.

Bain nodded. "That's exactly what I want you to do."

"You can't expect me to do that! She did exactly what she threatened to do!"

"Because you wouldn't change! But now look at you!"

Jake blinked and his lips parted as he glared at Bain in disbelief.

"You go to church!" Bain went on, trying to make Jake understand.

"I wouldn't say I've changed," Jake shook his head. "I just started going because I knew that's what she wanted."

"So, in other words," Bain said. "You're going to try and win her back."

Jake considered Bain's suspicions. Should he just go ahead and confess? That it started out that way but then he came to realize he needed it? No. Bain would think he was crazy.

"Yeah," Jake whispered. "That's exactly it."

He looked down. He wasn't going to admit that he now only had one beer a day, cutting back and trying to better himself. It's what Georgia would've wanted. And, to be honest, Jake didn't know if he was ready to see her again. He needed more time.

"But I'm not ready for her," Jake admitted softly. "I made a mistake by bringing her here so soon."

"You knocked her up!" Bain exclaimed. "It was the only thing you could do."

"She was just a child!" Jake defended himself, even though it didn't look or sound good for him. He was the one who was in the wrong! "And I was foolish. A twenty-year-old that was horny for a teenager!"

"Now, look at you." Bain tried to justify Jake's actions, taking a step towards him. "Taking responsibility. You've been raising your child all alone for almost six months now. And she deserves to see her mother again, Jake."

"She's a four-year-old who doesn't know what happened," Jake sighed. "She thinks Georgia is just around the corner!"

"And what if she was?" Bain said softly.

"Don't taunt me, Bain," Jake threatened with a growl.

Bain sighed, sagging under the weight of the situation. "You're right," he whispered. "You clearly need a little more time away from your wife."

Jake clenched his jaw, not liking that word. *Wife…*

He wasn't ready for one at such a young age. Five years apart, Jake had eyed Georgia when she still had a whole life ahead of her. But he'd wanted to get her away from the Mormon religion. It wound up following her here to their home and Jake had hated it when she would leave for church on Sundays. When she tried to change him and get him to go, he would blow up on her. He even hit her a couple times because she wouldn't stop. The first time she gave a warning that she would leave if he ever did it again.

He hadn't cared at the time, but then the second time had come… and she'd left like she'd said she would. Jake had gone after her just to watch her stray onto the road and get hit by a car. He thought she was dead, but still rushed her to the hospital. The memory haunted him.

Jake shook his head, being thrown into the memory of when he got the news. They had to cut into Georgia and do a liver transplant. She lost a lot of blood and her liver was dying from the impact of the car. Jake shuddered as he remembered how in love he was with the woman at the time. He'd been so stupid to ever push her away.

But, now… All he could think about was delivering the divorce papers to her. He still regretted hitting Georgia, though. He should *never* have laid a hand on her. Jake looked up at Bain after having a moment to himself, coming out of the memories.

"Can you do me a favor?" Jake asked quietly.

Bain nodded his head, watching his best friend.

"Could you call up your lawyer friend in Utah? I have some papers I want Georgia to sign."

Fear danced in Bain's eyes. "No. Jake. No… You need to think clearly here."

"I am."

"Blair needs her mother!"

"She'll get one." Jake defended himself. "It just won't be Georgia. I have someone else in mind."

"My sister is off the market, Jake! No!" Bain boomed, trying to get a point across.

"She needs her." Jake did his best to try and convince Bain. "Your sister is the only option."

"She's engaged! You're not ruining this for her!" Bain pointed at Jake threateningly. "Back off!"

"I need her. Bain," Jake insisted. "Blakely is my everything."

"Fuck off, Jake," Bain growled. "You already have a wife."
Jake glared at Bain.

"And if you want a divorce that bad, you'll deliver the papers to her yourself." Bain set a card and a small gift on the table. "Happy Birthday, Jake. Give Blair a hug for me." He walked out of the kitchen and Jake heard him walking out the front door a few minutes later. He wasn't coming back until Jake changed his mind, he knew that.

But Jake wasn't going to do that. He lifted his chin, not wanting to leave Blair to go get Georgia or just deliver the papers to her. If she didn't remember him, then why even go?

As if he'd summoned her with his thoughts, Blair walked into the kitchen, holding onto her stuffed teddy bear. She walked over to Jake and he bent down to look at her.

"Hey, sweetie," Jake whispered sweetly. "Did Uncle Bain wake you?"

Blair nodded her head. "Where's Mommy? Is she home yet?" Her sweet little voice broke Jake's heart at the words that came out of his mouth.

"No," he whispered. "And she won't be home for quite some time."

"I miss her." Blair put her lips to her teddy bear, her blue eyes on Jake. She looked so much like her mother, reminding Jake what he once had.

"Me, too," Jake lied. "Sweetie. Me too."

He pulled Blair into a hug and kissed her head. Considering that Bain wouldn't help him and reach out to his lawyer friend in Utah, Jake might have to go there himself. Maybe seeing Georgia could help Blair. But then again, if the woman couldn't remember the family she had in Alabama, it might break Blair's heart if she saw her. And that was something Jake couldn't stand seeing. He loved his daughter way too damn much to break her heart. And he didn't love Georgia enough to risk letting her see their daughter after all this time. Did she even know what she left behind?

*~*~*

Georgia looked out at the mountains, content with herself and relaxed after a stressful morning. "Mm," she moaned, knowing she needed this. The peace and quiet felt nice.

Sitting at the top of one mountain on the four-wheeler Georgia felt a little better as she enjoyed the view. There was nowhere else she wanted to be. She could stay up here for days! Feeling at peace, Georgia took a deep breath in.

She closed her eyes and, after holding her breath for a moment, she let it out and sighed heavily.

"Georgia," Avery said, out of breath.

Georgia jumped at the sudden company and looked at her best friend, who was hunched over the four-wheeler. Is she okay?

"Don't hike the mountains," Avery groaned. "That is *way* too much walking."

"Avery," Georgia sighed, growing concern as she watched her friend struggle for breath. "Your asthma-,"

"I'm fine," Avery's blue eyes met Georgia's brown eyes. "My legs are just sore."

"But…"

Avery held up her inhaler and a bottle of water. Georgia closed her mouth and watched her best friend use her inhaler and wait a moment before having the last gulp of water.

"You couldn't have hiked this whole mountain. It's only been a couple hours."

Avery nodded her head. "Trevor."

Georgia lifted an eyebrow.

"He brought his side by side and let me catch a ride until the turn back there."

"That's an hour walk!" Georgia exclaimed. "Here. Come sit with me."

Avery nodded her head and Georgia made room for her on the four-wheeler. They sat a little awkwardly, their hips almost joined, as they looked out at the scenery. Avery sighed and sagged after a moment, seeming to enjoy the moment.

"Beautiful," she whispered.

"Yeah," Georgia breathed.

Avery looked at Georgia. "How much trouble were you in?"

Georgia blinked, not wanting to think about it.

"I mean… Considering your dad's face he wasn't really happy when you bailed on him."

Georgia shook her head. "Just another argument about me eavesdropping. He's worried I'll get in trouble with the wrong people by doing that."

Avery nodded, considering it. "I can see that," she mumbled.

Georgia looked at Avery, suspicious that her best friend was starting to side with her dad. Did Avery have feelings for Stephen after all? Oh, Georgia hoped so. They deserved each other!

"Georgia, your dad loves you." Avery defended him. "And, so do I. I mean… You and I… We…"

Georgia nodded, knowing where Avery was going with this conversation. "Confessed our love for one another."

Aver pressed her shoulder into Georgia's. "Not that we're *in* love. We're straight. But when we got drunk that night, I swear I was telling the truth. You're my best friend. And you always will be. No matter what."

Georgia gave Avery a side smile. "I feel the same way, Ave. We're soulmates. Besties. And sisters."

Avery nodded her head. "Just don't tell your dad," she whispered.

"What do you mean," Georgia asked.

"Well, I suspect he's in love with me. Back there…" Avery shook her head. "He defended me. Broke it off with Marissa over a simple, dumb misunderstanding."

Georgia sighed and sagged.

"He does…" Avery searched Georgia's eyes. "Doesn't he?"

Slowly, Georgia nodded. "But you didn't hear it from me." She muttered.

"You have my word."

Georgia looked down at her lap. "If we weren't so close… Would you…"

"Sleep with your dad?" Avery finished for Georgia.

Georgia felt Avery's eyes on her, but didn't know what to say.

"Oh, totally!" Avery gushed. "He's hot!"

Georgia snorted and looked at Avery, wishing it would happen. "You have my blessing, Avery. You can have him."

Brown eyes met blue eyes as they both considered the possibility.

"I could never." Avery shook her head. "No. I couldn't do that to my best friend."

"If you two got married, it would be endless sleepovers, you know." Georgia teased, even though it did sound nice.

Avery's eyes brightened up. "Well, that would be the only reason I'd marry him," she laughed, leaning into Georgia. "But I could never betray our friendship like that, Georgie. It would just be too weird."

Georgia nodded, understanding what Avery meant. "He really loves you," she said lowly and softly.

Avery nodded and looked down. "Then I better break it to him," she mumbled. "Before tomorrow."

"I would."

Avery looked at Georgia and gave her a small smile. She leaned in and kissed Georgia's cheek sweetly. "Now," she said, "we need to find you a new man. Jake was a-."

"No." Georgia shook her head. "Mm mmm. You can't make me."

Avery looked at Georgia in disbelief. "But, Georgia. You need the best of the best!"

Georgia shook her head. "Not right now. We need to focus on you. Your bridal shower."

"Please, tell me you got me something good."

"Oh, yeah," Georgia nodded. "You're gonna love it. As long as you still want Ashton."

Avery nodded her head greedily. "Yes. Georgia, to know that it was just a misunderstanding between Marissa and me, I can get past it."

"Okay. Let's get back to planning, then."

Avery smiled brightly and her eyes danced in the sunlight. "Oh, I hope there's strippers."

Georgia leaned in towards Avery, lowering her voice. "Why do you think Trevor's here?"

Avery gasped dramatically. "That mountain man is a stripper?!"

"Ha!" Georgia smiled. "Only he and Russ know how! I asked them to give you a dance tomorrow."

"Yes!" Avery threw herself back as she pumped the air and Georgia caught her before she could fall.

This camping trip was turning around and Georgia was grateful for that. She knew the bridal shower was going to go well. And the next day! It'll be kind of like a bachelorette party! But with no booze. Georgia forgot to get at least wine.

# Chapter 4

Stephen tapped his foot, anxious for Georgia to get back. He needed to let her know he loved her. That she was the only daughter he ever wanted. If Rayleigh was still alive, she'd know what to say. But instead, Stephen was left to look up at the sky, hoping she was watching.

"Please help me find the right words, Ray," Stephen whispered softly. He had hopes she was listening. He could use her words of wisdom right about now. *Be gentle,* echoes in Stephen's mind. He heard the four-wheeler in the distance and a few moments later Georgia came into view with Avery sitting at her back.

Their expressions changed from happy to grim when they saw Stephen and he stood up, knowing some things were said about him. He just didn't know what. As Georgia pulled in Stephen's eyes met with Avery's. Brown collided with blue and Stephen was pulled into a trance, almost missing the hint in Avery's beautiful eyes.

Her beauty was like no one else's. Just like Rayleigh and Georgia. But she was different from Georgia. The way Stephen felt about Rayleigh was the same way he felt about this blond haired, blue eyed beautiful woman in front of him, who was just as rebellious as his wife. And she'd gotten his daughter in trouble with her a time or two. Or seven. Well… Eight, now. Stephen was the only one that was counting, though.

Avery leaned in towards Georgia and whispered in her ear, making Georgia snort. Stephen looked down, feeling self-conscious about the situation he was now in. He just broke it off with Marissa and who knew how Ashton was gonna take it! He and Marissa were close! Stephen couldn't say he was surprised that the two would pull something like that off! They always greeted each other with a kiss on the cheek. Their whole family did! They're very sweet towards each other and always look out for one another.

Stephen may have been a little harsh on Marissa for the misunderstanding. But he couldn't let her get away with it. Couldn't she see the similarities between Shad and Avery?! They almost look like twins! And given the fact that their mother froze her eggs with their father's semen inside, they very well could be, but with a two-year difference.

Georgia finally got off of the four-wheeler. Stephen cleared his throat to get her attention as she quietly conversed with the love of his life and they giggled. When he cleared his throat with persistence Georgia stopped giggling and looked up at her father.

"Georgia," Stephen started. "I have to apologize. Can we talk? In private, please?"

Georgia looked at Avery and her best friend gave her a small nod. "Fine," she whispered in a mumble.

Stephen stepped aside and let his only child go first. He followed her into the camper and closed the door behind him politely, watching her intently.

"Don't make this a habit during this camping trip, Dad," Georgia warned. She turned around to face him. "I wanna be able to enjoy myself and Avery's shower tomorrow."

Stephen snapped at hearing the news. Avery was going through with it?! Stephen couldn't bear the thought, putting him in a bad mood. He wanted Avery to be happy. But at what cost?

"Then don't disrespect me like you just did, again!" He yelled, unable to fight his temper. "Your insolence is not going to be tolerated! You understand me?!"

Georgia winced and looked down. "Well, excuse me," she whispered with an attitude.

"Hey!"

"Hay is for horses," Georgia snapped as she looked up at Stephen.

He gave her a glare.

"Dad, this camping trip is about Avery," Georgia reminded him. "She's getting married in a couple of weeks! She deserves an uneventful time."

"I know it's a big deal for her!" Stephen yelled. "But that also means you need to be on your best behavior! You're her maid of honor for crying out loud!"

"Don't!" Georgia thrusted her fists down by her sides. "Remind me of that, Dad! I have enough on my plate as it is!"

"Like what?" Stephen took a threatening step towards his daughter and got in her face, tilting his head to the side. "You have a job cleaning buildings for the county after hours. That's four hours tops! And you do nothing but chores during the day! Which, by the way, is only a few!"

"I'm cooking dinner before I leave for work!"

"With laundry on Tuesdays and taking care of the animals every day! That's not very many!" "I'm cleaning the house, Dad!"

"You don't have to do that every day!" Stephen snapped. "Now, do you?!"

"Dad, stop!" Tears formed in Georgia's eyes as she started showing signs of getting offended. "I'm doing a lot," she whispered. She shook her head as she fought back the tears.

Stephen's heart broke for his daughter, seeing her cry had never been easy for him to see. Especially, when it was his doing. He took a step back, regretting his words. But was he too late to apologize?

"I do have to clean the house every day. I sweep, mop, do laundry, clean the kitchen, clean the bedrooms, do dishes, vacuum the house, and clean the bathrooms. I wash windows when they get dirty and the only time I have to myself is at night after I get home from work." Georgia sighed. "Where… I'm practically doing everything there, too. I'm cleaning bathrooms and break rooms, vacuuming rooms, washing windows, and taking out all the trash. And I'm taking care of three buildings right now because Nel is sick. So, don't get me started on not doing enough!"

Stephen sagged as he gave Georgia space. Working late and going straight to bed, he never noticed that his daughter was coming home later. He shook his head as he started to realize he was being too harsh on her. She *was* doing a lot. And Stephen wasn't giving her enough credit. As much as he loved his daughter, he wasn't recognizing all of her work. But it was no excuse for her behavior earlier.

"Don't eavesdrop," Stephen put in. "That's all I ask."

"Avery is my best friend," Georgia growled through her teeth. "I wasn't going to let her have that conversation with Marissa alone."

"She wasn't alone." Stephen sneered, taking a step towards his beloved child. "I was right there."

"You do realize she's not going to love you back?" Georgia snapped, unable to resist trying to hurt him.

Stephen froze, glaring at her.

"She's in love with Ashton," Georgia insisted. "Marissa's nephew."

"Don't remind me," Stephen grumbled, trying to forget. But Georgia had to break his heart.

"Then find a spot with service and call her up," Georgia suggested. "Tell her that you're sorry. Cause Avery is irrevocably, madly in love with Ashton."

Stephen grabbed Georgia's hip and kissed her forehead. "I'll never love anyone like I loved your mother," he mumbled, resting his forehead on Georgia's. "But that doesn't mean I won't stop loving Avery just as much."

Georgia shoved Stephen off of her with disgust. Their twin eyes met and he saw why she shoved him off. Her heart was breaking in her eyes and there was nothing he could do to stop it. He could tell it was for him. There was no one else she should feel that way for.

"Georgia," Stephen breathed as he started to pick up the hints. "You didn't."

"She was suspicious, Dad. So, she asked."

"Oh, Georgie," Stephen shook his head. "You shouldn't have said anything."

"I didn't have to," Georgia mumbled.

Stephen's heart shattered into a million pieces. She knew and she didn't return the feelings. Stephen didn't know what to do. All he knew was he was going to have to face her sometime soon. And since her parents were coming up today, he got a break from her tonight since she would be in their trailer.

But he wouldn't be alone to think, not with Georgia back in her original bedroom with him. They always shared a room whenever the family needed the beds in the toy hauler. And Stephen's sister was coming with her husband, so they'd be taking the back for some privacy. The bed the dinner table turned into was more for kids and the hide-away bed in the couch got in the way of the bathroom.

Stephen pulled his head back, not wanting his daughter to see his tears. She didn't need to see them. She didn't need to know how broken he was at the news of this newfound unrequited love.

Without warning Georgia hugged him. He looked at her, surprised at the action, but then

Stephen wrapped his arms around her and kissed the top of her head, grateful for the change. But how long was it going to last? Just a day? Stephen didn't know. All he knew was he had to embrace the change and enjoy it while it lasted.

# Chapter 5

Georgia laughed at Trevor, who was making an impression of a comedian. She didn't know who the comedian was, had never heard of his name before. But she bet her cousin was impersonating him to the tee. He could usually do that with celebrities they both knew!

Georgia covered her mouth as her other cousin, Trevor's older sister Taelynn, laughed at her laugh. Taelynn loved Georgia's laugh and always thought it was contagious. Georgia's laugh was high-pitched. And when she laughed even harder, she was wheezing to the point where only dogs could hear her!

Stephen joined in, giggling at his daughter, too. She looked up at him, sitting right next to him in his two-person chair that he used to share with her mom. Looking at Stephen was a wrong move, making Georgia laugh harder. She hid her face behind her hands, but he took the one closest to him, trying to make her look at him. She couldn't do it. It would just get worse!

"Look at me, Georgie," Stephen teased.

She shook her head, unable to do what he asked. She was somehow in the hyper stage of tired.

"Look at me, sweetheart."

"No."

"Why not?"

Georgia set her elbow on the arm rest as she kept her face hidden. "Because I can't."

"Why?" Stephen dragged out.

"You'll make me laugh!"

Stephen giggled. "Then look at me," he teased breathlessly.

"No!" Georgia took her hand back from her dad and covered her face for a moment longer. Then she aimed her face away from everyone and looked out at the scenery with her chin on her palm and her finger over her top lip.

Trevor started mooing like the comedian did in his bit he shared. Georgia snorted and covered her face. But she was getting over her laughing fit. Stephen joined in on the mooing and it just about put Georgia into another laughing matter. But she restrained herself.

"Are you done yet," Georgia asked.

"No," Stephen replied quickly.

"Here," Russ, Georgia's other best friend, put in. "I got this."

"No, you don't," Georgia slyly dismissed him.

He bent down next to her and their eyes met. Brown looked into dark-green and Russ started giving Georgia teasing, seductive looks. He lifted his eyebrows before he started hitting on her.

"Hey, sweetheart," Russ said smoothly, clearly hitting on his best friend of ten years. "Wanna give me a ride?"

"Oh, pfft!" Georgia looked away as she held back a laugh. She wasn't giving into it! There wasn't a chance Russ was going to succeed this time!

"I'll give you one if you'll give me one," he continued as he slipped into the teasing tone of voice he'd picked up from his friend Jay. Years ago, they'd kissed while playing spin the bottle - and even after Russ had told Jay he was straight, they'd stayed close friends.

Russ was now married with two kids of his own. But when Georgia asked him to give Avery a show for her bridal shower, he couldn't say no. Georgia was just glad that Russ's kids were at his parents' house.

"Come on, baby," Russ continued in the same teasing voice. "You know you want me."

Georgia buried her face in her dad's chest as she burst out laughing and the rumble from his laugh made her laugh even harder. She could never get past that line for some reason! Taelynn started laughing and Trevor was on the verge.

"How do you do that so well," Trevor asked through his laugh. "I mean… I can do a decent flirty voice, but yours is truly authentic."

"I have a gay best friend," Russ replied.

"That explains it," Trevor nodded.

Georgia moaned into Stephen's chest as she started to come to, but it was hard when his laugh was contagious. After a moment as Trevor and Russ picked up a conversation Stephen started to come to, helping Georgia get over her giddiness.

A few minutes went by as they calmed down to quiet and Georgia kept her face in her dad's chest. Feeling his hard chest under her face she got reminded of how much he worked out. And she remembered why all of her friends had a crush on him.

Could she maybe change Avery's mind about him? Would a date spark interest in her? There was no reason for it to not happen. Stephen was clearly madly, irrevocably, uncontrollably in love with Avery. But she didn't return the feelings. Georgia wanted to make her dad happy, no matter how many times he made her angry in just one day. She loved him. He's the best dad she could ever ask for, even when he was doing the bare minimum for her. But sometimes…it was hard to love him.

Georgia didn't know what happened five years ago.

Why she left or where she went. All she could remember was leaving Alabama after waking up in a strange house. Georgia had grabbed the keys that were on the counter along with what looked like her wallet, a bag of her clothes in hand. She was told she ran off with a twenty-year old after saying bye to her friends and leaving her dad all alone. He'd found Marissa while she was gone, but apparently, she was gone for *five years.*

What happened in those years? Did she get married? Have a life of her own? Did she go to school in Alabama? Georgia may never know. But she felt as though the scar on her stomach was the key to the answers she was looking for. Should she look into it? Or should she let it slide? If that

Jacob guy abused Georgia, she didn't want to find out the truth.

Stephen rubbed Georgia's back, bringing her out of her daze. His lips landed on the top of her head. His hand stopped on her shoulder blades. And that was when she realized he was cherishing the moment. She couldn't help but reciprocate in the littlest way she could find. Letting him love on her like a father would with his daughter. They had a moment before they're brought out of it by an approaching vehicle.

"Shit," Trevor said lowly.

Georgia looked at Trevor as Stephen stiffened. "What is it?"

Trevor motioned at the truck that pulled up with his head. "Ashton."

Georgia quickly got up, knowing what must've happened. Marissa had called him. That had to be the reason why he was a day early – he wasn't supposed to be here until after the bridal shower!

Georgia turned to face Ashton, who was sitting in his blue truck and glaring right at

Stephen. He stood in front of Georgia to protect her. But it wasn't her that Stephen needed to worry about. It was himself. Georgia started for Ashton as he slowly got out of his truck. She made it half-way before he stalked forward and towards Stephen.

"Ashton, wait." Georgia tried to stop the Olympic track runner, but he pushed past her. "Ashton!" She turned towards him and watched him as he slammed his fist into the side of her dad's face.

Trevor and Russ instantly got up to defend Stephen as he went down, but Ashton ignored them as he looked down on Stephen.

"A 'misunderstanding'," Ashton snapped. "When we thought she was cheating on me! I didn't realize Marissa thought it was Shad until I got his name! You should be ashamed of yourself!" Ashton pointed at Stephen. "You should never have had a chance with my aunt! You're a disgrace!"

Trevor started for Ashton, but Georgia hurried over to stop him. She set her hands on his chest, but she forgot about Russ, who stalked over to Ashton to defend Stephen.

"I better not find out you're in love with my fiancé or it's hell for you!" Ashton went on, yelling louder.

"Russ, no!" Georgia screamed for her best friend to stop, but he reached over and grabbed Ashton by the shirt with his fist pulled back. He stopped and looked at Georgia, their eyes meeting across the way. She shook her head at him.

"Don't make it worse than it is," she begged. "Please."

Russ took a moment then shoved Ashton off. Ashton looked over at Avery, who was helping her parents set up their trailer and things.

"Avery," Ashton barked, his voice unsteady.

It sounded like Russ shook him. And Georgia didn't blame him. Russ was a big guy along with Trevor and Stephen. But Russ was a bodybuilder more than Trevor and Stephen, who were more of mountain men than Russ. They most definitely had their differences.

"Let's go," Ashton ordered his beloved fiancé. "We're not staying."

Avery stood up, looking at him. Her eyes met Georgia's. Georgia gave her a slow shake of her head. Avery looked at Ashton as he stalked for his truck. "I can't."

Ashton stopped where he was and looked at her.

"My bridal shower is tomorrow," Avery reminded him. "Everyone's gonna be here. And it's too late to cancel."

"This man is practically in love with you," Ashton snapped, pointing towards Stephen.

Trevor and Russ helped Stephen up behind Georgia as she protected her most beloved father. She wasn't about to let Ashton deliver another blow!

"If you return the feelings, then be my guest. Stay," Ashton growled. "Or you can come with me… Your fiancé that I hope you love… And we can host your bridal shower somewhere else up here. But I'm not letting Stephen Rhinehart near you. You understand me?"

Avery looked over at Georgia and mouthed *"I'm sorry"* before starting for her fiancé.

"Avery," Georgia started. Her soft gaze met Avery's apologetic gaze. "I'll see you tomorrow."

Avery nodded her head before getting in Ashton's truck. He closed the door after holding it open for her. He stalked over to the driver's seat and got in, slamming the door before starting his truck. Georgia started to look back at her dad to check on him. But she suddenly felt his presence behind her and she was comforted to know he was okay.

# Chapter 6

Stephen looked up at Russ to discover he was handing a bag of ice to him. He took it, his cheek and jaw sore with a pulsing pain. He was lucky Ashton hadn't knocked out a tooth. Or at least loosen one. But to double check, Stephen ran his tongue along his teeth. He would need to make sure he didn't have a concussion. Have someone ask him some questions.

Georgia set her hand on his back as he settled the side of his face into the ice pack, his elbow on his knee. She looked at him with worry.

"I'm so sorry, Dad," Georgia whispered. "That was uncalled for."

"I deserved it," Stephen grumbled. "Ashton had a point." Comforted to know he still had all of his teeth, Stephen looked at his daughter. He needed her more than ever right now. "I just got angry about what he and Marissa did to Avery."

"With good reason," Georgia mumbled.

Grateful for her secrecy, Stephen gave her a forgiving look. He owed her a lot for this. And he was going to start tonight.

"We're so sorry, Stephen," Nayla, Avery's mother, spoke up in front of him.
He looked up at her.

"Ashton was out of line," she went on.

"Yeah," Stephen whispered, deciding to avoid eye contact with Nayla.

"But is it true?" She asked. "You're in love with our daughter?"

Stephen couldn't look Nayla nor her husband in the eye, but he still looked up at them anyway. "I am."

"Well, this is awkward," Lionel, Nayla's husband, said. "If you married her, you could be my son-in-law. And I'm only a year older than you!"

Stephen snorted at the obscenity that was clearly not going to happen. "Well, you don't have to worry about that."

"Oh, come now," Nayla waved off the obscenity in a dismissive gesture. "You're an amazing man. And our daughter would be lucky to have you. Besides! It would give us a reason to hang out more and go on more camping trips together."

"Yeah, if you wanted me to tag along," Georgia said in a teasing disapproving tone.

Nayla smacked her lips together, sounding like a horse, as she looked at Georgia. "We love you. Stop it."

Georgia looked up at Nayla. "Then I wanna declare my love," she started in an enthusiastic, dramatic, and teasing tone. "For *you*, Lionel."

Russ snorted and laughed, apparently knowing an inside joke. Stephen caught on after a moment, realizing that Georgia was reversing the unrequited love he had for Avery. Knowing his daughter was doing this to enlighten the mood and make him feel better he couldn't be prouder.

"Don't tempt me, Georgia," Lionel teased. "I'm not that old and could still sweep you off your feet if you let me."

"Oh, I have a crush on someone else." Georgia waved off the idea. "And he's my age." She looked over at Russ as she sat down and winked at him. "Well… He's two years older. But you get the point."

Apparently, Russ knew something and Stephen wanted to know who this guy that Georgia had a crush on was. He knew it was a subject women talked about, but Stephen wanted to be a part of Georgia's life and be someone she trusted. He hoped that she would tell him someday. He knew it wouldn't be today unless it slipped out somehow.

"And who is this mystery guy?" Lionel asked, interested to know what Stephen was interested in more than anything. He sat down in front of Georgia, his eyes on her.

"See, I couldn't tell you that," Georgia teased. "Because if I did, I'd have to kill you."

Stephen snorted, but he still gave Georgia his disciplinary tone. "Georgia," he dragged out.

"Sorry, Dad," she shook her head. "But I couldn't tell you either."

Stephen's eyes narrowed. "I'll get it out of you one way or another."

Nayla started humming a tune. Stephen looked at her with a teasing glare. He knew that song. And it was so Nayla to hum a tune she got reminded of by just a few words.

She and Stephen had grown up together and stayed good friends. They never saw each other as more than friends, which was why Stephen could talk to her so freely. Nayla knew Stephen's past. Their eyes met.

"Hm?" Nayla raised an eyebrow and Stephen looked at his daughter, dismissing his best friend.

He picked up on the conversation Georgia was having with Lionel and he joined in. Georgia shook her head as Avery's dad tried to guess who Georgia's crush was.

"You're not gonna get it," Georgia giggled. "It's none of those men."

"Well, then give me something," Lionel said excitedly. "Not just brown hair and brown eyes! That's more than half the population!"

"He works out."

"Your dad."

Georgia snorted and put her face in her hands, which were in her lap. Stephen went red, embarrassed that Lionel would think a daughter would have a crush on her dad. "Maybe when I was four!" Georgia squeaked, embarrassed. She lifted her head for a quick moment before covering her face with her hands, again.

Stephen looked at his daughter in dumbstruck awe. She couldn't be serious! I mean… Every woman's first crush might have been her father when she was a baby or toddler, but she would never admit it! Especially, this one! When she was a baby, it was always Mom, Mom, Mom. Never Dad. And when she was a toddler, she was still so attached to her mom! Dad couldn't help her with anything! Stephen felt flushed in the face and Nayla laughed, her eyes on him.

"Who else could it be," Lionel asked as everyone but Stephen laughed.

He didn't know what to do. Or what to say! Was he supposed to discipline his daughter for telling such a deep secret? He couldn't do that! This was an honest, fun conversation where everyone was supposed to guess who Georgia's crush was.

"My brother," Russ finally spoke up. "Jensen."

Stephen looked over at Russ and their eyes met. This was the secret! Georgia had a crush on a military man! Russ dipped his head to Stephen, acknowledging his past in the army. Jensen was following his father's footsteps, a man Stephen served with. Luckily, he made it out alive.

"Georgia has a crush on a warrior," Nayla asked, sounding impressed. She nudged Stephen and he looked at her. "She's got good taste." Nayla wiggled her eyebrows at Stephen.

He smiled, flattered at Nayla's compliment. Georgia finally looked up and her eyes trailed to Russ, who met her gaze with confidence.

"I'm gonna kill you later," she threatened her best friend.

"Georgia!" Stephen snapped, his glare on his daughter. Brown eyes met brown eyes.

"Well, now it's gonna get around!" She yelled. "I can't afford the humiliation!"

Nayla sighed. "She's right. Jensen is a decorated soldier." She closed her mouth and acted like she was zipping it up, drawing her fingers across her lips. "My lips are sealed."

Georgia nodded her head. "Thank you, Nayla."

Nayla gave Georgia a reassuring squeeze. "You. Are. Welcome. Sweetheart."

Lionel snorted. "This is a perfect opportunity to tease! I mean… Jensen? He's a hero! And Georgia deserves someone no less! We gotta hook 'em up!"

Stephen nodded his head, proud of his daughter for eyeing one of the good ones this time. Jake had been such a bad choice. "I agree. Georgia and Jensen would be perfect."

"Georgia is right here!" Georgia squeaked for the second time.

Stephen looked at her and squeezed her knee. "I just want you to be happy."

"I can't believe you actually agree to this. After everything you told me when I was little."

"Ah, come on," Stephen breathed. "I was just joking."

"'*Marrying a military man puts your life on the line,*'" Georgia impersonated her father, lowering her voice. "'*I did that to your mother and I regret it. I almost lost her because of some enemies I made.*'"

"You make enemies wherever you go," Lionel put in. "I'm one to talk since I do business with the military on the side. But I've got family and friends that made enemies at their normal jobs."

Georgia nodded her head. Stephen patted her knee to get her attention. Looking into her eyes he knew she was afraid to love the military man she had a crush on. He had to help her see that it would be okay to love a military man. Just like her mom had loved Stephen.


*~*~*

Stephen looked up at the ceiling, unable to sleep, again.

But this time, for a whole entirely different reason. Georgia was asleep next to him, and he was worried. For her. She had a crush. And she didn't want to act on it. How could Stephen help her see that it was okay?

Loving a military man was no different than loving an ordinary man. It just meant more fear that he would be coming home in pieces. Stephen saw a lot of wounded and dead as a doctor for the army. But he never had to worry for Rayleigh and Georgia getting the news. He stayed safe for the most part. There was only one time where he thought he was going to die. And that was when his base swas attacked by terrorists. Not wanting to think about it, Stephen tried not to hear the echo of guns and screams. But he was thrown into the memory without warning.

*Stephen was running across the field again to get to safety. He knew how to use a gun. He knew how to fight. But violence was something he wanted to try and avoid. He had people to save! Pain surged in his thigh and that was when Stephen realized he was shot. He went down on his knees, clutching onto his bleeding thigh. He looked at his hand to see how bad the wound was. And that was when he noticed a bullet from a sniper. That man needed to be taken out. He lifted his gun and looked around for the sniper. Looking up at the roofs he didn't see anything at first. But once he turned towards the medical building there she was. She? Shit… This wasn't going to end well. Stephen took the shot and the sniper thrust her head back before lying on the roof on her side. He got her. But when he got up pain surged through his hip and he went down. Fuck!*

Georgia rolled into Stephen, bringing him out of his memory. She snuggled into him for the very first time and he looked at her in shock. Something had changed. And he had to admit he liked it.

"Thanks for not embarrassing me earlier," Georgia mumbled.

Stephen stifled a laugh, knowing what she was talking about. "How could I? It was news to me."

"Oh, what. Ever."

"Georgie, you were all about mom. I couldn't even look at you! All through life it was 'Mom, Dad's looking at me, again'," Stephen said in a high-pitched voice, staying quiet enough not to wake his sister and brother-in-law.

Georgia snorted. "Because you were always giving me that look," she giggled.

"What look?"

"The one that said 'clean your god damn room'," she explained.

Stephen snorted and stifled a laugh. "That's not what I was thinking."

"Then what were you thinking?"

"How beautiful you were," Stephen whispered.

Georgia looked up at him and their eyes met.

"And how I wished you would let me near you," Stephen admitted. "You were so much of a momma's girl."

Georgia snorted. She kissed Stephen's cheek for the very first time, letting him take the moment to kiss her cheek. He closed his eyes as he enjoyed the warmth Georgia offered. She rested her chin on Stephen's chest and her bangs fell in front of her face.

"All I've got is you," Georgia said softly. "I can't afford to lose my dad at a time like this."

Stephen kissed Georgia's forehead. "You'll never lose me, sweetie," he whispered against her head.

Georgia nodded, snuggling in with Stephen to rest her head on his chest. He got comfortable with her and he was able to fall asleep in just minutes with her in his arms.

# Chapter 7

Georgia woke up refreshed and stretched, rolling into her dad. That was the best sleep that she ever had while camping! She couldn't believe she slept all through the night! Stephen yawned as Georgia rested her head on his chest and his hand trailed up her arm.

"How'd you sleep, sweetie," Stephen asked through a haze, clearing his throat.

"Like a baby," Georgia whispered.

"Good," he whispered. A moment of him tickling her arm went by.

Georgia enjoyed the contact, wishing it would happen more. Stephen had said she hated him growing up. But what he didn't realize was that he was always gone, working in the army and hardly having time for her and her mom. When he did come home, he was always distant, not all there in their play time.

Georgia had learned just to brush it off, but she wished she had had a dad growing up. She admired her mom for sticking with him. But she didn't think she could do that with Jensen. She'd have too hard of a time with it. Stephen rolled on top of Georgia instantly, startling her and pinning her arms to the bed.

"Quick," Stephen said in a rush. "What's the first thing you do when a man tries to attack you?"

"Nail 'im in the balls," Georgia retorted, seconds before she punched her dad in the junk and he grunted.

He doubled over on top of her as he held his private parts. "Not me, you dumb dumb."

"Ha!" Georgia laughed. "That's what they all say."

Stephen pinched Georgia's side, getting a scream out of her. She kicked her leg, trying to get him off of her. But then she remembered her aunt and uncle asleep in the back. She cringed. Would they be able to hear her? Stephen giggled in Georgia's ear. He nodded his head in victory.

"That's right, Georgia," Stephen said softly. He rocked his hips as he straddled his daughter. "You just fell right in my trap."

Georgia shook her head as she looked up at the off-white ceiling, wondering if it was actually once white. "No," she mumbled. "I just remembered Aunt Colleen and Uncle Rye are here."

"Shit," Stephen pulled back to look at Georgia. "You're right."

"You just swore."

"You swear all the time," Stephen narrowed his eyes at Georgia. He motioned his chin at her. "It's no different."

Georgia snorted.

"You two are so cute when you get along," a familiar female voice said from behind Stephen.

He cringed and stiffened at the sound of his sister's voice.

"I love it," Colleen went on, "but it's weird that you're straddling her, Stephen."

"Right." Stephen got off of Georgia and the bed, backing up to stand next to Colleen. He looked at her. "Sorry," he whispered. "I got carried away."

"I'd say!" Colleen laughed.

Georgia got up on her elbows and looked up at Colleen. "Wanna get some fresh air?"

Colleen looked at Georgia with a bright smile. "I would love to!"

Georgia nodded. "Just let me get some clothes on."

Colleen looked at Stephen, gesturing to his bare chest. "Some of us need to put more on." She teased.

"Warm night," Stephen crossed his arms. "Sorry."

"You couldn't have snuggled with your daughter?" Colleen asked. "She looked like she was freezing!"

"It was cold," Georgia agreed.

Stephen looked at her with a glare of disbelief. "If you took the time, you'd know I'm a heater. Use that info as you will."

"Thanks, Dad."

"Good," Stephen nodded. "Now, I'm going to get dressed."

Georgia looked up at Colleen. "Is the back open?"

Colleen's blue eyes pierced Georgia's brown eyes with a teasing look. "You'll have to fight Rye for it. He's currently doing the same. And he forgot underwear."

"Oh!" Mortified, Georgia did her best to get the picture out of her head. "I'll just change in here, then."

"With your father?" Colleen asked in surprise.

Georgia nodded. "There's a hiding spot in here that I've used before."

"Don't let him peek when you're just in a shirt and panties," Colleen agreed hesitantly. "He'll look to see if you got the same birthmark as your mother and tease you about it."

Georgia snorted.

"He did that with me when we spotted our mother's birthmark when we were young." Colleen explained. "Except it was on her shoulder."

Georgia put her hand over her mouth as she laughed. "He hasn't said anything yet!"

Colleen's face dropped. "And I just gave him the idea."

Stephen got giddy, rubbing his palms together and looking at Georgia with a grin on his face. She shook her head at him, telling him not to do it. He nodded his head at her, eager to look. Where was the birthmark on her mom? She hoped it wasn't the ass, where her birthmark was.

"I'm gonna change in the bathroom," Georgia spoke up after her silent disagreement with her father.

"Good luck," Colleen put in. She walked out of the trailer, making it shake, then closed the door behind her.

Stephen raised his eyebrows at Georgia. "Let's see that birthmark," he teased.

"Nope." Georgia got up and raced for the bathroom, bumping into her dad.

"Oh, come on!" He said, sounding disappointed. "You're no fun, Georgia!"

Georgia opened the door to the bathroom and saw her dad getting naked in her peripheral vision. Disgust and awkwardness took over and she quickly ducked into the bathroom. In her haste she'd forgotten to grab her clothes, but she could act like she was going to the bathroom.

After a moment, the back door opened and the pump turned on. The bathroom door opened and Georgia looked up in the face of her Uncle Rye. Oh, shit…

"Sorry, Rye," she breathed as she walked out.

"Wha," Rye started. "What were you doing in there?"

"Hiding from my dad." Georgia opened her dad's bedroom door and covered her eyes, not wanting to see anything. She felt for her bag and grabbed it as she heard Rye laugh behind her.

"Oh, kids," Rye dragged out happily. The bathroom door closed and Georgia knew it was safe to go in the back. But her dad grabbed her and thrust her down onto the bed.

"Dad," Georgia yelled. "No!"

"Your mother gave birth and I was right there to see it," Stephen exclaimed. "I can see your ass one last time!"

"No," Georgia screamed, her panties were yanked down and she tried to get up, but she got pinned down and she screamed out again in protest.

"Yep," Stephen said quietly as he put Georgia's panties back over her ass. He sounded a little mortified. "You got it."

"Stephen! Rick! Rhinehart!" Georgia flipped onto her ass and backed up on the bed.

Stephen looked at her with a smile on his face. He giggled. "You actually listen."

"Stay away from me." Georgia held her hand out in front of her, her palm facing her dad as her eyes pierced his eyes. "No, touchy, touchy."

Stephen snorted. For some reason Georgia had to look. Still dressed in just jeans without a shirt on, Stephen looked good. And Georgia had to make the look quick. She noticed a bulge and she wished she hadn't looked. Why did her dad have a boner?! Did he have a sex dream last night?

"I saw that, little missy," Stephen said in his distasteful tone.

"Saw what?" Georgia asked plainly. She swallowed to try and moisten her dry throat.

"You checking me out."

Georgia gave her father an attitude, looking at him through slitted eyes. "I would *never*." She stuck her tongue out at him and he leaned over to flick it with his pointer finger, keeping eye contact with her.

"Good," he said. "Cause I didn't raise my daughter to be into incest."

"Oh, yeah," Georgia scoffed sarcastically. "Cause you were there every day."

"Watch it, Georgia May Rhinehart." Stephen snapped, glaring at her with his hands on his hips.

"I'm just saying." Georgia brought her knees up to her chest and hugged them, looking at the wall. "I saw mom every day while you were gone. It killed her to see you leave and have her raise me all by herself while you were gone on those tours. You didn't raise me. Mom did. Which is why I won't do anything about my crush on Jensen. I can't be with someone in the military."

Stephen sighed heavily. "I'm sorry," he whispered. His fingers brushed Georgia's bangs back. "I really am."

Georgia shook her head, looking out the window and somewhat see through blinds. They were white and if you stood close to them, you could see in or out. Stephen's lips landed on Georgia's temple lovingly.

"I never meant for you to think that way," Stephen mumbled softly.

"But you did." Georgia looked into Stephen's eyes, his face so close to hers. Her lips almost brushed his. And it was kind of weird, but in a way it was also comforting to  have her dad so close. He was always so far away because of work.

Georgia didn't know what she would do if he didn't love her. What would've happened if he didn't take her back when she came looking for him a few months ago? Would he have kicked her out? Oh, Georgia hoped not. She couldn't afford to be out on her own right now. She needed her dad now more than anything. Even when he was being an ass. He's the only thing she's got beside her two best friends.

# Chapter 8

Jake walked out the front door with Blair in his arms and locked it. Usually, he didn't bother to lock his door when he left but he was going to be gone for a while and he couldn't afford a burglary. He wasn't all that rich, working a blue-collar job to get by. But if all went well, his business would be taking off soon. And it would do him some good with that extra money. He'd even be able to start a college fund for Blair!

"Why can't I come with," Blair asked Jake.

"Because mommy and I need to have a chat," Jake replied, starting for the truck. "A long-needed chat."

"I could play with my cousins while you chat," Blair suggested.

"Oh, sweetie." Jake's heart broke for his daughter. He so wished Georgia had siblings. His brother and sister had spoiled Blair with a lot of cousins! And he couldn't be more grateful for such a big family that was still growing. But sadly, that's not the case with Georgia. "She doesn't have any nieces or nephews."

"Why?" Blair's little voice sounded so innocent and sincere.

And it made Jake want to hold her close. "She doesn't have any siblings."

"Oh." Blair nodded. "What are siblings?"

"Sisters and brothers," Jake explained.

Blair nodded her head as Jake put her in her car seat. "And sisters and brothers make babies with their spouse."

"That's right." Jake nodded, after he got Blair buckled in.

"And a spouse is someone like mommy." Jake looked at Blair.

"Someone you love and marry."

Jake nodded his head, wishing he could say he still loved Georgia. But they fought so much that in the end he fell out of love with her. He'd probably regret that later.

"Yeah," Jake drew out, unsure and nervous. He didn't want to say it. He didn't want to tell his daughter he didn't love her mom anymore and break her heart even more. She deserved to see Georgia one more time.

"Where you going?" Bain asked, appearing next to Jake and making him jump.

Blair laughed as Jake glared at his best friend. "Utah."

"Oh, good," Bain said. "Send a post card, will you, please? Sis wants to go there, again."

Jake shook his head as he tightened Blair's seatbelt. "It's Mormonville. I'm not doing such a thing."

"Ah," Bain dragged out. "No, it's not. Georgia once told me there's a lot of people there falling away to a different religion."

Jake closed the back door.

"Please say you're taking Blair with you," Bain said. "It would be good for her."

"She's staying at Mom's and Dads," Jake explained. "I've already talked to them about it."

"And so did I," Bain grinned. "You're taking Blair with you."

"Forget it," Jake shook his head. "I'm not putting her through that pain."

Bain shrugged in confusion. "What pain?"

"You said so yourself," Jake reminded him. "Georgia doesn't remember."

"And seeing Blair might spart something!" Bain defended himself as Jake started for the driver's seat of his black truck. "Come on, Jake."

Jake opened the door and looked at his best friend, someone who was like a brother to him.

"Take her with you," Bain pleaded.

"I don't have a plane ticket for her," Jake mumbled.

Bain handed him an envelope. "I took the liberty to get her a seat right next to you."

Jake took the envelope and looked inside of it. His plane ticket was in there alongside a new one for Blair. "Bain," he growled. "I can't just take her."

"You can," Bain nodded his head briefly. "And you will. Now, let me take you."

Jake reached into his truck and grabbed the file from the top of the console in the middle of the two front seats. He showed it to Bain, who looked at it funny before it hit him. He stared at Jake, distraught.

"No," Brain dragged out. "Jake, it'll kill her."

"Blair. Not Georgia," Jake started. "And I'm just doing what's best at this point."

"What's best is for you to get your head out of your ass and into the big picture." Bain insisted, getting in Jake's space. "You need to save your marriage," he snapped quietly. "Not break it! Don't end it, Jake." Bain pleaded with his brother. They weren't related by blood. But they were best friends.

"I have to," Jake grumbled.

Bain growled in annoyance.

"What else am I supposed to do?" Jake asked. "Have sex with her?"

"No," Bain snapped. He closed his mouth and looked away, clearly pissed off but he was trying to control his anger. He clenched his jaw and looked at Jake after a moment. He shook his head in silence. "Please, don't end it, Jake. Georgia deserves the benefit of the doubt."

Jake leaned forwards, towards Bain. "What she deserves is freedom. And she's not going to remember any of this no matter how hard Blair and I try. I'm taking advantage of her brain injury from the accident and delivering the divorce papers." Jake put the file back in his truck. "You can't stop me."

Bain looked around Jake and at the file. Jake knew what he was thinking. And it wasn't going to happen. Bain lunged forward, but Jake held him back as he reached for the file.

"No!"

Bain grabbed Jake by the shirt and pushed forward, backing his best friend since birth up. Jake may not be little anymore, but he sure felt like it while he pushed against his friend that was a body builder! Damn, he was big! Jake dug his heels into the ground and pushed back into Bain. They wrestled for the upper hand and Bain wound up winning, shoving Jake into the truck and grabbing the file.

He tore it in half, looking Jake in the eyes. Then he tore the halves in half. Great… Now, Jake had to talk to his lawyer again before he left!

"Fuck you, Bain," Jake snapped, getting in his brother's space threateningly. "That was my only way out."

"More like the easy way out," Bain replied coldly. "And that's not going to happen."

"Bain!"

"You two love each other! Deserve each other!"

"I don't love her!" Jake yelled in Bain's face.

Bain glared at him, his piercing blue eyes looking almost identical to Jake's today. Jake took a moment as he realized he just spilled the beans in front of his little bean, taking a step back from Bain. The man threw the torn-up file on the ground.

"Then you're falling in love with her," Bain growled. "All over, again. Because she's the best sister-in-law we could ever ask for. Even if we're not really related." Bain bumped Jake in the shoulder as he walked away, leaving his best friend to clean up the mess he made.

Jake sighed, bending down to pick up all the pieces. After that he threw it in the garbage. Jake pulled his phone out of his back pocket and called up his lawyer. It rang three times before he picked up.

"This is Analdo," Analdo answered.

"Hey, Analdo," Jake started. "This is Jake. Jacob Farr."

Analdo was quiet for a moment.

"Listen," Jake sighed, "is there any way for me to get another copy of those divorce papers?"

"Look in your mailbox," Analdo said. "There should be another copy in there."

"Thank you. I truly appreciate it."

"You're welcome, Mister Farr."

Jake hung up the phone, walked over to his mailbox, and opened it to find a file in there. He pulled it out and looked at it, making sure it was what he needed. Once he was satisfied with his findings, he walked over to the truck and got in the driver's seat. When he heard sniffling from the back seat, he looked in the rear-view mirror. Seeing his daughter crying, he looked back at her.

"Sweetie, what's wrong?" Jake asked in concern.

"You don't love mommy," Blair said in her sweet voice. She truly sounded heartbroken and Jake wanted to fix that.

"Oh, honey," he cooed. He reached back and grabbed her calf. "Sometimes people fall out of love."

"Yeah, but… Not you and mommy," Blair sniffed. "You were always together. Happy and mad. Sappy and sad."

"She left me first, baby," he mumbled. "And we're going to see her one last time."

Blair shook her head. "I don't wanna go. Please, don't make me."

"What changed your mind?" Jake asked. "You wanted to go just a few minutes ago."

"That was before I found out you don't love mommy," Blair said. "You're getting divorced." She sounded unsure of what that meant, but she knew it was bad.

Jake sighed heavily, knowing where this was going. And if he didn't say or do the right thing, he could ruin his relationship with his beloved daughter. Just like Stephen did with Georgia when she talked to him about leaving home with Jake.

"I don't wanna be a part of that," Blair almost whispered. "I just want mom."

*Fuck…* Jake was losing his daughter already. How could he turn this around?

"Daddy loves you, sweetie," he whispered lovingly. "And I will never let you go like mommy did."

"From what I heard from Uncle Bain say she doesn't even remember us," Blair said. "And I bet if she saw me, she'd remember me."

"Oh, baby," Jake whispers. "It wouldn't work like that."

"Take me to mommy," Blair said. "Then I want you to leave. I only want her." She was confused, going from one decision to another.

Jake squeezed Blair's thigh but she shoved his hand off of her. He looked out the windshield, his heart breaking. Great… His family was falling apart and it was all his fault.

# Chapter 9

Avery looked into the gift bag in her lap and pulled out teddy lingerie. She instantly went red as gasps were heard in the crowd. Oh, dear. Maybe Georgia should've waited until Nayla wasn't looking! Avery's cousin, Kaylee, leaned forward.

"You're gonna look sooo good in that," she spoke up. "Black is your color."

"Oh, no," Avery's sister, Hannah, added, coming towards Avery. "She looks good in baby blue."

"It's true." Georgia looked at Kaylee. "Baby blue complements her very well. Black is just a distraction."

A snort is heard, but Georgia can't pinpoint who was the culprit. She looked around the group of people that were gathered for the bridal shower. Her eyes landed on Avery's older cousin, but the woman shook her head at Georgia and pointed out the culprit. Avery's other best friend. Georgia narrowed her eyes at Dayna, who opened her arms in an *'I don't know'* motion with her eyes in slits, teasing.

"What?" Georgia asked teasingly. "You think she looks better in black?"

"I was actually agreeing," Dayna started. "I can't see Avery in any other color. Which makes me wonder why you got black?"

Georgia smiled. "You should see the underwear that goes with it."

Dayna blinked in surprise. "Oh!" She looked at Avery as the lucky bride pulled out the baby blue underwear that went with the teddy. "Oh, my! Georgia! Those two colors are ravishing!"

Georgia shrugged her shoulders as she batted her eyelashes flirtatiously at Dayna. "Thank you." She said with a teasing tone, even though she was flattered.

Dayna snorted again, but Georgia ignored her. Hannah laughed while Nayla started to go red, her eyes wide as it finally registered. Her eyes snapped on Georgia.

"Georgie," Nayla breathed. "Really?"

Georgia nodded her head, a smile on her face. When Nayla started to flush, Georgia giggled.

"Put it away, Avery," Hannah said, sounding more giddy than urgent. "You're gonna give mom a heart attack."

Georgia burst out laughing, leaning forward in her chair. She couldn't believe the scene that was unfolding all because of lingerie!

"Georgia," Avery's long-lost aunt spoke up. "What made you think Avery wanted a teddy?"

Georgia watched the woman as she got up and grabbed the present she brought for Avery's bridal shower. Their eyes met and all Georgia saw were stars and laughter in the woman's eyes.

What was her name, again? Georgia swore she forgot it all the time! Isn't she someone's mom? Someone Georgia knew? She looked familiar for some reason.

"Why not?" Georgia shrugged.

The woman quirked the corner of her lips in a sly, teasing grin. She didn't do anything further. She just gave Avery her present and sat down to watch. Avery pulled out the tissue paper first. Then came a Ramona mesh plunge bra with a matching mesh thong, a Ramona garter belt, and thigh highs to go with the set. Georgia's jaw dropped at the baby blue color and how it was see-through. And she thought she knew lingerie for Avery!

"Bella," Nayla snapped. "For my daughter?!"

That's what it was! Her name was Bella! Georgia looked between the sisters as they started to bicker.

"What?" Bella defended herself. "It's just lingerie!"

"That could scar my husband if he ever saw it!"

Bella started giggling uncontrollably, Shyla, Nayla's other sister, sitting next to her with a big grin.

"No!" Nayla pointed at Bella. "It's not funny!"

"Oh, but it is," Bella laughed.

"We're talking in private later."

Bella blew a raspberry at Nayla with her tongue sticking out. "That just means I won."

"Oo," Nayla growled.

Georgia heard a man laughing behind her and she looked back over her shoulder and up to see Ashton arriving a little too early. What was he doing here? He'd already caused enough trouble!

"Ready to go, babe," he asked Avery. "I just made a phone call for us to rent a couple jet skis."

Avery hurried over next to Georgia. "We were just getting started. We've only visited for thirty minutes and are just getting around to opening presents."

"And it seemed I missed the good part," he teased. "All I saw when I pulled up was a bra!" He snickered.

Georgia snorted and pressed her lips together, holding back a laugh.

"That's for later." Avery reached out and leaned into Georgia's chair. "I need more time. Please."

Ashton turned to Georgia. "Could you bring my fiancé to Bear Lake once you guys are done here?"

Georgia nodded her head, eager to get Ashton out of here before her dad got back. He left for fishing this morning with her Uncle Rye after their talk and she knew he would be back with his catch soon.

"I got your number," Georgia put in.

"Good," Ashton nodded. "Thank you."

"You're welcome."

Ashton walked over to his truck and Avery bent down to talk to Georgia. Their eyes met.

"Whatever you do," Avery whispered. "Don't call him. All he'll do is talk bad about your dad."

Georgia nodded her head. "Then you better be the one to call him while we're on the road."

"Okay," Avery nodded her head in agreement. She stood up and sauntered back over to her chair. She grabbed a present that hasn't been opened yet and sat down. Her delicate fingers got under the lip of the wrapping paper and she gently pulled it back. She unwrapped the present to reveal a boxed kitchenette. She showed it off, grateful that her other aunt got her something sensible.

Stephen pulled his line in, a fish caught on his hook.

He'd caught quite a few fish while the women were at the bridal shower in the campground. It was his plan to fish the whole entire time. He wanted to help set everything up, but he also wanted to avoid Avery.

She didn't love him. He could tell in her eyes when she came back with Georgia on the four-wheeler. She was in love with Ashton. Stephen would never gain her love. And he hated it.

The fish flopped out of the water, revealing its size. A good-sized river fish, Stephen could tell by its length and heaviness it was at least seven pounds. That's a pretty dang good fish! He reeled in his catch, standing in a shallow spot of the river.

Stephen quickly caught the trout in his hand and put the fishing pole in between his knees. He gently reached one finger into the fish's throat, where it swallowed the hook. He felt for where the hook got the poor fish and, with a flick of his finger, got the hook out just enough before having to use his tool that can do the rest of the job.

He heard someone wading in the water behind him, but he didn't look back at them. He already knew who it was. "Hey, Wynston."

"I see you caught a few," Wynston's familiar low voice replied.

"Yep," Stephen drew out. "I just couldn't go back to the camping spot yet."

"Ah. Bridal shower."

Stephen nodded his head. He finally got the hook out of the beautiful cutthroat trout and put his tool back in his tackle box. "Have you talked to Samantha?" Stephen bent down as the fish thrashed from side to side, eager to get away from him. He gently kept a hold as he lowered it into the water.

"Not a word," Wynston replied.

"Good." Stephen let the fish go and it swam away. He grabbed his rope with his three dead fish and turned around to look at the man responsible for the woman's attack. Maybe he hadn't attacked her himself, maybe he'd even really loved her, but he still put her in a situation that no man ever should.

"She deserves better than you," Stephen reminded him.

Wynston glared at Stephen. "Listen-,"

"No. You've already tried to explain yourself." Stephen looked at Wynston and shook his head at the man. "It just made you sound worse."

"But if you could just-."

"Understand?" Stephen cut Wynston off, getting worked up. "What's there to understand? She trusted you. You went running somewhere you weren't familiar with and decided to take a 'shortcut'." Stephen air quoted. "You just about got her killed. You're lucky that man and his friend were there."

Wynston winced. He looked at Stephen's fish, his DNR badge on his chest for everyone to see. "You won't mind if I search you for more fish, then." It was a statement. A tone that Stephen never liked in anyone.

Stephen glared at Wynston. "You think I would go past the limit?"

Wynston shook his head and looked at Stephen. "I'm letting it go that you got three."

"I wasn't able to save the third one." Stephen defended himself. "And three's the limit!"

"Then let me search your box."

Stephen scoffed in disgust. But he did what he was asked. He tossed his tackle box to the man that broke Stephen's niece's heart. If it wasn't for him, she would still be here. She wouldn't have run off to another state. "You're doing this because I'm the only one that hasn't blocked you."

"I'm doing this because it's my job," Wynston snapped as he zipped and unzipped pockets on Stephen's tackle box, searching it thoroughly.

"Keep telling yourself that, Wynston." Stephen shook his head, watching the DNR policeman. "But we both know why you're really doing this. You wanna punish me. The family. For pushing you out of our lives!"

Wynston finished his search and glared at the older man in front of him. "I had no idea it was such a bad area!"

Stephen waded through the shallow water, stalking towards Wynston. He took his box from him with a glare. "Samantha told you before you booked the hotel." He growled through his teeth.

He grabbed his tackle box from Wynston, who handed it to him. He stalked over to the riverbank then started for the campground. He knew it was safe to go back. The women should be done with the bridal shower and Stephen should be safe from Avery. She'd be with Ashton. Stephen made the little trek to his truck without any incident and put his fish in the cooler.

He set his fishing pole and tackle box next to the cooler in the bed then got in the driver's seat. He started his truck, not much on his mind. At the age of forty-seven you learn to ignore drama and stay out of it. You also learn to keep your mind clear of unnecessary thoughts. It comes with practice throughout your younger years. And Stephen could tell you that it was worth it.

He pulled out onto the road after checking for clearance and slowly got to the campsite, the drive only taking ten minutes since he didn't have to go very far for a good spot. Stephen bought this land. And even though he owned it he still had to abide by the fishing rules for the river. He didn't own it.

Once Stephen got to the campsite, he pulled up next to his trailer. The women were cleaning up and Nayla was spotted sneaking two gift bags away from Avery. Stephen snorted and shook his head.

Nayla was just like her mother, taking the lingerie away until the honeymoon. Nayla's mom always got beat red over lingerie, not wanting to have to think about her daughters doing the deed before the big day. Luckily, Nayla's sisters were all happily married.

And her mom could rest easily, knowing Nayla and Shyla would take after her. Bella is more rebellious and doesn't care what her daughters get for their bridal showers. Stephen got out of his truck. Georgia met him and he took a step back to give her space.

"I need to use your truck," Georgia started. "I have to take Avery into town."

"Fine," he whispered. He put his keys in his daughter's hand. "Don't wreck it. Please."

"I'll be careful," Georgia nodded. "Like always."

Stephen snorted and stifled a laugh. "You?"

Georgia furrowed her eyebrows at Stephen.

"Georgia, last time I let you drive you backed into the trailer."

"I was fifteen!" Georgia tried to defend herself.

"That was three days ago," he reminded her. "Right before we came up here."

Georgia smacked her lips in defeat. "Fine." She put the keys in Stephen's hand. "But don't let Ashton see you."

"Thank you." Stephen got back in his truck and Georgia got in the front passenger's seat.

Avery got in the back seat and put her seatbelt on right away. "Georgia, I don't like this."

"My dad had a point," Georgia sighed. "I'm not used to driving something so big."

"I am," Avery snapped.

"It's my truck," Stephen put in, defending himself. He looked back at the young woman he knew he was going to have to get over. "My rules."

Avery sighed and slunk back in the seat. She pouted, her bottom lip sticking out. Stephen ignored her the best he could, knowing she was doing it to get her way. Usually, he would fall for it. And he wanted to. He wanted to trust Avery. But she chose Ashton over Stephen, knowing how he felt about her.

He doubted it would be any different if she found out from him. He knew her. If she made a decision after finding out one way, there was no way her decision would've changed in a different situation. Stephen started his truck, backed it up onto the dirt road, then started down it towards the paved road that led to Bear Lake.

The drive was awkward.

Quiet without anyone saying anything. Stephen left the radio off for what seemed to be thirty minutes of driving. Once he got on the paved road a squeak came out of Avery.

He glanced back at her to find one hand over her mouth and the other covering her crotch. Georgia pulled her visor down and looked into the mirror as Stephen looked out of the windshield. He didn't want to think about why Avery did that. She was a woman. It could be multiple reasons!

It was quiet, again, as Stephen drove. After driving for another thirty minutes, they were out of the canyon. Phones in the truck started going off and Stephen grabbed his to see if he had any missed calls. Two. A text came in, but he didn't look at it. Instead, he kept his eyes on the road and set his phone aside. Georgia and Avery were texting away on their phones. Stephen knew they were conversing without having to ask them. He knew the girls like the back of his hand.

Georgia snorted. Her fingers flew across the screen of her phone. Stephen didn't know what she was talking about with Avery. And he didn't want to find out. He cleared his throat before starting a conversation.

"Where am I dropping you off?" Stephen finally asked.

"The gas station at the light," Georgia replied. "I just got a text from Ashton."

Stephen nodded his head. He cringed at hearing Ashton's name, but he knew it was normal. When you're in love it's hard to hear another man's name. Especially, if he was dating the woman you loved. But in Stephen's case Ashton and Avery were getting married. In just two weeks.

Stephen did his best not to let his heart get the best of him. But he still wanted the woman that was there for him while Georgia was gone. She did a lot for him. And to think that she didn't feel a thing for him… It broke him to a million pieces. Stephen wanted to break Avery's heart to show her how he felt. But he knew she would never love him. And that was the toughest part to get over.

And if anything were to happen to Georgia… Stephen would be completely alone.

He wouldn't have anyone to share the grief with. Stephen drove down the winding road. He passed houses, a fun place with slip n' slides, a go-cart ring, and a jungle gym outside while there was who knows what inside. It didn't take long before he was passing the gas station that was right in front of town and he was slowing down more. This was a spot truckers have had their breaks go out. It was tragic every time, the truck going into houses at the light since it was unable to stop on its own. The city decided not to build there since the last incident.

Stephen shook his head as he got closer to the light just to notice something going up. A business. It wouldn't last long if a truck's brakes went out! The people of the homes that were destroyed were lucky none of them were there! Stephen pulled into a parking spot next to the gas station at the light and Avery quickly got out.

Georgia stayed in the truck, her nose buried in her phone. What was she doing? Why wasn't she getting out? Stephen cleared his throat.

"Georgie," he started. "Why aren't you getting out?"

"Cause I was just supposed to drop Avery off," Georgia replied. She sounded urgent. Uneasy. "Can we go, now?"

"Georgie," Stephen dragged out. "What aren't you telling me?"

Georgia went quiet, her thumb swiping on the screen it was hovering over.

"Georgia."

"If you don't leave now, Ashton will try to beat your ass."

Stephen laughed, throwing his head back. He truly thought it was because Georgia didn't want to be spotted with him. In a way she didn't. But to find out it was because of Ashton, Stephen couldn't help but howl at the obscenity. He looked at Georgia after a moment, seeing the uneasiness on her face.

"I can take care of my own," Stephen replied. "I don't need you to defend me. Even though it's nice."

"It's not that," Georgia trailed off. "It's Ashton. He couldn't take you on even in a million years! You'd kill him!"

Knowing his past, Georgia knew he fought in Afghanistan when he was in the army. Three tours. And they felt like they lasted a lifetime, making Stephen miss most of Georgia's childhood. "So, you're worried about your best friend's fiancé more than me."

Georgia nodded her head, her soft, worried brown eyes on her dad. "I know what you can do," she breathed.

Stephen nodded his head, understanding where Georgia was coming from. He cleared the frog out of his throat before continuing. "Okay. We'll leave. But can we go get our burgers and shakes first?"

"Yeah," Georgia whispered. "That sounds great actually."

Stephen nodded before putting his truck in reverse.

# Chapter 10

Georgia picked at her Little Bear Burger, taking it apart and just eating the pickles.

She wasn't very hungry, still full from the food at the bridal shower. But she couldn't deny her dad a daddy-daughter date. Not only did he deserve the break, so did she. Georgia was able to slip a tampon to Avery before she slipped away with Ashton. When they went over that bump Avery had a little accident. Georgia was just glad she was prepared.

She slowly ate her burger and fries, but she highly considered taking it back to the campsite. It wouldn't be a bad idea.

"You full from the shower?" Stephen asked.

Georgia nodded her head. "I kind of ate a lot." She admitted, not wanting to lie to her beloved dad.

"Then save it for later."

Agreeing with her dad, Georgia put the bun back on the top and wrapped it up in the paper it came in. She then grabbed her chocolate raspberry malt shake and slowly ate it, savoring every bite. She could never resist something as good as this.

"Listen. Georgie."

Georgia looked up at her dad and their twin eyes met.

"I don't know what happened with Avery while you two were on the four-wheeler," he said. "But I'm not happy that you told her."

"Dad, I didn't say a thing."

"Georgia," Stephen drew out, warning his daughter.

"She just had her suspicions!" Georgia insisted. "She caught on and I never confirmed nor denied it. And I said exactly that."

Stephen sighed and sagged while Georgia shook her head at him.

"I'm sorry, Dad," she said. "But she just doesn't feel the same way."

"I wish she did," Stephen said lowly. "But no one can force anyone to feel a certain way."

Georgia's heart broke for her dad. She knew he loved Avery greatly. She could tell by the way he looked at her best friend. She wished Avery loved him. He deserved the best in life and Georgia believed that was Avery. But maybe someone else would come along and steal Stephen's breath away. Someone closer to his age.

"Stephen," a mature female voice asked. "Stephen Rhinehart, is that you?"

Stephen perked up at the voice and instantly stood up. "Amanda Murks!"

He smiled brightly at the blond in front of him, who was standing next to a young man. Stephen hugged the woman tightly and Georgia's eyes met with the young man's.

He raised an eyebrow at her and she stood up, drawn to his quirkiness.

"How's it been?" Stephen asked.

"Oh," Amanda, the woman, dragged out. "I can't even start!" She set her hand on the young man's arm. "This is my youngest. He just got back from a mission."

Stephen looked at Amanda's son. "Well, congratulations."

The man looked at Stephen. "Thank you."

"Where did you go?"

"North Carolina."

"Beautiful state."

The man nodded his head in agreement. "Indeed, the mountains are really something over there." He looked at Georgia. "Is this your daughter?"

"Yes." Stephen set his hand on Amanda's elbow, lightly grabbing it to get her attention. "Amanda, this is Georgia. My one and only daughter."

Amanda gasped, gaining Georgia's attention. "You look so much like your mother. Rayleigh and I go way back."

"How far back?" Georgia found herself asking.

"All the way to grade school. We met in kindergarten, but hated each other then. We both liked your father." Amanda set her arm on Stephen's shoulder, her blue eyes on Georgia. "I, of course, lost. But Rayleigh and I had a mutual understanding and became good friends in junior high."

"And who is this?" She pointed at Amanda's son.

"Oh, this is Gavin," Amanada smiled. "Watch out. He might pull you in without warning. He does that to women."

"Thanks for the heads up," Georgia laughed, knowing it's already happened.

"I think I know who you married," Stephen started teasingly. "Sounds like Gavin is a mini me of him."

"Ethan is lucky I gave him another shot," Amanda agreed.

"How did that go?" Stephen asked. "I don't see a ring on your finger."

"Sadly, we got divorced," Amanda explained. "While Gavin was away on his mission."

"That had to be tough," Stephen looked at Gavin. "I'm so sorry."

Gavin nodded his head. "I'm getting through it." He looked at Georgia. "But I would get through it better if I had someone close to talk to." He seemed to be genuine.

Just like Amanda warned, Georgia was drawn into Gavin. The two of them stepped aside so two old friends could catch up and they got to talking.

"I don't know anything about divorce," Georgia started. "But I have a friend that does. He's up at the campground, but I'm sure he'll come join us at some point. You could talk to him."

Gavin shook his head. "I'm good. Thank you, though." He took a step towards Georgia. "I mean… It would be nice to talk to him. Find out how he got through it. But…"

"You're behind closed walls right now," Georgia mumbled.

Gavin nodded his head, his hands in his pockets. If he was a mini version of a friend of Stephen's, Georgia could get in on that. Gavin was deliciously handsome. His dark hair was swept to the side while his hard figure was outlined with muscle.

Georgia had always had a thing for tough boys. It didn't matter if they were military boys or biker boys. She always had to be by one. She knew Gavin must've been grieving the loss of a connection with his dad. But if his dad was biker or military, Georgia wanted a chance at him. Forget men her age! She wanted older! Gavin nodded his head at Georgia.

"I think I changed my mind," Gavin started. "I want you to call your friend up to see if he's here yet."

"Of course," she breathed. She pulled her phone out and called Russ up. It rang three times before he finally answered. "You must be in Bear Lake."

"Actually, I'm in the mountains," Russ replied teasingly on the other end of the phone.

"Ha, ha," she laughed. "Very funny."

Russ snorted.

"I've got a new friend that would love to meet you," she explained. "His parents got a divorce while he was on his mission and he just got back."

"Where did he go?"

"North Carolina."

"Please, don't tell me it's Gavin Ellertson," Russ groaned. "That poor guy was all over the place on his mission."

Georgia lowered her voice. "It's Gavin."

Russ sighed into the phone. "I'm on my way there. Don't. Let him out of your sight. He was suicidal and I don't know how he is, now."

"You have my word," Georgia promised. "Thank you."

"You're welcome." Georgia hung up the phone and looked up at Gavin. "Good news. You met him on your mission."

Gavin perked up. "Is it Russ? He was so good to me. Better than my companion."

Georgia nodded her head. "He was in South Carolina. So, how did you guys meet on your missions?"

"I was being transferred over to South Carolina. And while I was there for just one week, Russ was there to help me out," Gavin explained. "I couldn't thank him enough. He got me out of my hell hole before I was sent back to North Carolina with a new companion that was actually a good one."

"Was your old one…"

"Abusive?" Gavin nodded his head. "My mission president saw me with new bruises and black eyes every week."

"I am so sorry," Georgia whispered.

"Thank you," Gavin mumbled. "I could use a couple friends like you and Russ. I don't think I'd survive without friends right now."

Georgia nodded her head. New plan. Become friends with Gavin and meet his dad when they go to his place. That way Georgia could meet Ethan and get her way with him.

She wanted him in bed. She wanted him on the kitchen counter. She wanted the man that created this beautiful specimen to give her beautiful babies of her own.

Georgia's eyes faltered. She found herself checking Gavin out but she didn't find a bulge on him. Oh… She was hoping to get one out of his dad. Georgia looked up as she realized why she was thinking like this, her hormones were raging. She was right to bring tampons with her, handing one to Avery earlier when she needed it. Georgia was glad she brought a bunch. She was going to need them.

*~*~*

Russ met up with Georgia and Stephen at the burger stand, Gavin and Amanda already hanging out with them. Stephen and Amanda were talking up a storm, catching up, as Georgia and Gavin sat to the side and listened.

"The moment Rayleigh caught on it was too late," Stephen said. "I already made the deal."

Amanda laughed. "The poor girl!"

Stephen nodded in agreement. "I felt bad. But we got a good deal out of that house and we were both happy."

Amanda smiled. "I'm glad it worked out for you two."

"Me too," Stephen whispered, looking down at his now empty bag that once held his burger and fries.

Georgia looked at Russ as he sat next to her, food in hand. "You're late," she said.

He looked at her. "Not as late as your sorry ass."

"Hey!"

"Hay is for horses."

Gavin laughed and Russ and Georgia looked at him. "Sorry," he waved them off. "But you just reminded me of an inside joke my girlfriend and I have."

Georgia smiled. "You have a girlfriend?"

Gavin nodded. "She's amazing. Been really good help since the day I left for my mission."

"Oh, you're still with her?" Russ spoke up next to Georgia, looking over her head.

Gavin looked at him. "Yeah."

"Congratulations, man." Russ reached around Georgia to shake Gavin's hand. "That's the longest relationship I've ever seen anyone in. Ten years sure is a long time."

Gavin nodded. "Thanks, man. Yeah, my parents were only together for twenty-one years. It's still a world record for them, though. I've never seen them get along much."

"That has to be tough," Russ said softly, sounding sincere.

"Very much so." Gavin had the last bite of his milkshake before continuing. "I wish they could've lasted."

"I wished the same with my parents for a while, too," Russ agreed. "Mine got divorced before I left for my mission. It was tough. But I got through it."

Gavin looked at Russ. "Have your parents found anyone new?"

"My mom found someone permanent while my dad has a new girlfriend every week," Russ explained.

Gavin made a sound of disgusted uncertainty, twisting his lips and gritting his teeth. He shook his head. "See, my dad had an affair with a new girlfriend every month!"

"Ouch!"

Georgia got up and started cleaning up the garbage, knowing Russ and Gavin needed to catch up. A male hand landed on her lower back and she looked up to see Trevor had joined the party with his wife and daughter, Jackie. He put his lips to her ear.

"Your bra strap is showing," he mumbled.

"Oh!" Georgia looked at her shoulders before fixing her shirt. "Thank you."

"You're welcome." He pulled back, looking at her. "Are we heading over to the lake? Jackie wants to swim."

Georgia nodded, looking up at her cousin. "Yeah."

Taelynn joined the group with her husband and two girls, carrying food.

"Well, you guys have been here for a bit."

Taelynn looked at Georgia. "We went to a different burger stand. It was less busy."

"That's not LaBeau's."

"Oh, no," Taelynn shook her head. "They're way too crowded."

Georgia nodded her head, knowing how the burger stand was. People loved it so much, it was always slammed with business. "Well, we're gonna head over to the lake once my dad and his new girlfriend are done talking."

"*Friend*," Stephen defended himself. "Old friend."

Georgia looked at him.

"And you should remember that for next time."

Georgia dipped her eyebrows towards the bridge of her nose in a furrow, challenging her dad.

"Stephen," Amanda said softly, grabbing his attention. "Be careful what you wish for." She teased in a breath.

Georgia laughed, knowing where Amanda was going. She and Stephen must've talked about going on a date. He nodded his head.

"My bad, Manda." He leaned in towards her teasingly. "I don't wanna mess up our dating plans, now do I?"

Amanda nodded in agreement, keeping her eyes locked on Stephen. "You better remember that," she said in a whisper.

Georgia laughed evilly, unable to hold back her new motive. Gavin may be gorgeous, but she planned on making him her step-brother. Talking to him made her realize she wished she had one and this was the perfect chance to make it happen.

Stephen looked up at her.

"*No*," he warned, dragging the word out. "You're not doing anything."

Georgia raised a brow challengingly. "Make me," she teased in a whisper. Oh, she was so totally going to get her dad and Amanda to fall in love! It was the perfect plan!

# Chapter 11

Jake pulled into Stephen's driveway, risking a beating from the man in front of his daughter. But when Jake discovered the lights were off in the house in the setting sun, he knew Stephen and Georgia weren't home.

Usually, Georgia would be in the kitchen at about this time, cooking dinner with her music blasting on her phone through her Bluetooth speaker. Stephen would have the garage door open as he just got home from work. But the house was quiet.

Jake was safe. For now. But who knew when Stephen and Georgia would be back. They must be out camping, Stephen's truck missing from the side of the house. If Jake were to go to the backyard, would the camp trailer be there? He sighed and sagged.

He didn't want to trespass, but he had to know where Georgia was. A few loud knocks sounded on his window, making him jump. He looked to see Stephen's neighbor. He rolled down his window to say hi to the woman that was always over when Rayleigh was alive. The two of them were best friends no matter their age gap. "Hey, Cathy," Jake started.

"They're not home," Cathy replied. She put her hands on her hips, her blue eyes piercing Jake's blue eyes. "They've gone camping."

"How long were they gonna be up there for?"

"I'm house sitting for another four days. Stephen missed Georgia and rightfully so. Don't you dare kidnap her, again," she threatened.

"I didn't kidnap your bonus daughter, Cathy," he groaned.

"She's not my bonus daughter." Cathy took a step away as she pulled her cardigan into her. "Granddaughter is more like it."

"My apologies." Jake put the car in park. "But I need to speak with Georgia. And if you're not going to tell me where exactly-."

"Why do you need to speak to Georgie?" Cathy pressed, showing that she was not very happy to see Jake back home.
"I need her to sign divorce papers."

"Oh, thank the heavens above," Cathy dragged out, throwing her head back and looking up to the sky. "Hallelujah!" She looked at Jake. "We can get rid of ya for good!"

"Just point me to the canyon Georgia's in," Jake sighed.

"She's at Franklin Basin. Now, get out of here before I chase you out." Cathy's southern accent never left her. She sounded redneck more than ever, but that just made Jake miss home.

He nodded his head briefly. "Yes, ma'am."

"Sounds like you went to the south," she said.

"I did." Jake put the car in reverse and looked at Cathy as he started backwards.

"Well, stay there," she snapped. "We don't want you knockin' Georgia up, again. That was a mistake you two made."

"I tried to make it right, you know," Jake insisted.

"Oh, boohoo." Cathy followed Jake to the road, wrapping her cardigan around her body. "That doesn't justify anything!"

Jake blew a raspberry at Cathy, sticking his tongue out at her in irritance. "Thanks, Mom."

"Careful," Cathy warned. "Your real mother's up there with them. Avery's getting married in a couple weeks."

"So, I've heard," Jake rolled his eyes.

"Oh, come on," Cathy raised an eyebrow at Jake as he sat in the road in his rental car. "Be happy for your cousin."

"How can I?" Jake asked. "She chased me away!"

"For good reason."

Jake moaned in disgust. He looked out the windshield. "And for your information." He looked at Cathy. "My real mom disowned me."

"We all did, Jake," she snapped. "You raped Georgia."

Jake shook his head. "It wasn't forced."

"But you're still five years apart."

"So, she was fifteen!" Jake yelled. "And I was twenty! Big deal!"

"It is a big deal." Cathy got in Jake's face. "Now, get out of here." She spat, hatred in her eyes. "We don't want you here and we *never* will. Jacob."

"Daddy?" Blair asked from the back.

The look on Cathy's face changed as she winced. She went quiet. "No," she whispered.

"She delivered." Jake mumbled. "And I was the only one there for her."

Cathy glared at Jake. "Oh, fuck you!" She spat. "I heard my sister was there! She took you in!"

"She took Georgia in," Jake snapped.

"Well, I hope she wins your little one in the settlement," Cathy swent on. "And I wish you ill will."

"Thanks, Cathy," Jake smiled. "You sound just like my mother."

"She forgave you," Cathy called as Jake raced down the street, Blair crying in the back.

"It's okay, Bee," Jake cooed. "Don't believe a single word that woman said. I didn't do anything mean to your mom."

"Are you sure?" Blair's little voice sounded scared. She couldn't be scared! She should be comforted with her dad so close!

Why did Jake let Cathy continue with the insults? He should've stopped her before she said anything crude! Jake looked his daughter in the eye through the rear-view mirror.

"I promise you, baby," Jake said soothingly. "I would never hurt Mommy."

"Then please tell me you love her," Blair pressed. "Please, tell me that what you said this morning was a lie."

Jake couldn't do that. But he knew he had to somehow muster it. He couldn't lie to Blair. Not after the truth came out. He just. Couldn't. Do it. Blair started crying in the back, closing her eyes.

"Blair, baby," Jake started. But he knew he couldn't comfort her. Not in this subject. Not in the way she wanted. He reached back to touch Blair's leg, hoping he could provide something for her.

"No," Blair screamed as she shoved Jake's hand off of her. "I don't want you!"

Jake looked at her in the rear-view mirror with broken eyes.

"I want Mommy! And only Mommy! You mean nothing to me!"

"Bee… You don't mean that."

"I do mean it! I mean every word!"

Tears welled in Jake's eyes as his heart broke. His family was breaking apart. And there was nothing he could do about it. Could he love Georgia, again? No. He didn't think so. But he just might have to try to mend his family back together. For Blair. It seemed like it didn't matter what Jake wanted at this point. But he was still going to try for a divorce. For him.

*~*~*

Georgia stretched in her chair after having such a delicious dutch oven dinner. Those potatoes were amazing. Russ's lips landed on her ear as she rolled towards him in the two-person chair they were sitting in together.

"Want some peach cobbler," Russ asked teasingly.

"Don't tempt me," Georgia mumbled.

Russ snorted and pulled away from Georgia. His arm draped over her shoulders as she slunk into the chair.

Georgia and Russ had been best friends ever since kindergarten. They had the kind of friendship where they saw each other as brother and sister. Since Georgia was the only child in her family, Russ stepped in as the big brother role. And he was the best big brother Georgia could ever ask for. Even though he was just two months older than her. Avery, who was sitting across from Georgia at the other side of the firepit, was that sister Georgia always wanted. Stephen walked over to the fire and dropped a piece of wood in.

He stoked it, wearing a glove, and moved pieces around. Georgia watched him as sleep started to creep into her mind.

To be honest, she still kind of had a crush on her dad. Seeing him with just pants on this morning renewed it. But she would never act on it. Georgia wasn't into incest. And neither was her dad. They both strongly believed in love with strangers or friends. Which was why Georgia was glad to see Stephen smiling and laughing with that Amanda woman.

She so would've loved seeing Stephen happy with Avery. But that was out the window now. Avery was going to ignore her feelings for Georgia's dad. Georgia knew Avery felt something for him. But she wasn't going to push it. If Avery wanted him, she would do something about it before it was too late. Georgia nudged Stephen with her foot and he gave her a warning glare.

"Georgia, I love you," Stephen started. "But I will throw a coal at you if you try to push me into this fire."

Georgia snorted. She raised an eyebrow at him, egging him on. "Do it, I dare you." Stephen slapped Georgia's foot away as she tried to nudge him again.

"Ow!" Georgia stuttered. She set her foot down, knowing better than to urge her dad forward. If she did, she'd get it when they got in bed tonight.

"Anybody interested in some peach cobbler," Russ asked. "I could use something sweet."

"You can't make me make it," Avery defended herself.

Georgia was proud of Avery. She decided to stay and face the awkwardness with Stephen. Who knew how the night was going to end. But at least Avery would be in Nayla and Lionel's trailer if she decided to sleep here tonight. Nayla set a dutch oven over the fire and gave her daughter the look.

"You're lucky I made it then," Nayla replied coolly.

Georgia sat up. She watched Russ as he got up and walked over to his trailer. He went inside, turned a light on, then disappeared around the corner of the window. Stephen sat next to Georgia and draped his arm over her shoulders.

"What are you thinking?" Stephen muttered in Georgia's ear.

"Nothing," she murmured. She didn't want to tell her dad how horny she was. That she wanted to nail Amanda's ex all night long. She was still trying to forget how beautiful Gavin was, but only seeing him as a friend.

She could still see him when she closed her eyes. His dark hair was in a beautiful boy cut, his long bangs barely hanging over his forehead. His blue eyes pierced Georgia's brown eyes and looked into her soul.

When Russ had shown up, Gavin's eyes lit up and the two talked like old friends. They avoided the conversation about their missions, Russ knowing what happened since Gavin was so open to him. Georgia never would've known

Gavin was such an open guy with his past. He seemed to be the type that would close it all up.

Boy, was Georgia wrong. If she were to tell you about something in her past, you would have to be her best friend. Someone she could go to about anything. Someone she could trust. Georgia found herself clenching her thighs together as she got wet down there.

She *hated* this time of the month. She got so horny it was hard to ignore! She didn't know how she was going to survive tonight. Sleeping next to her dad was going to be a challenge. What if she needed to relieve herself in the middle of the night? Would she wake him up with her pants and moans as she pleasured herself? Oh, she hoped she could at least ignore it until morning. She didn't want her dad to hear her.

# Chapter 12

Stephen woke to a car pulling up, its headlights shining bright outside. Great. Colleen and Rye were going to get woken up, now. Who was coming? The bridal shower was over with! But then, again, the bachelorette party was today. It was Sunday, now, right?

Groggily, Stephen grabbed his phone and looked at the time. It was barely midnight. Who's here, then? None of Avery's friends were coming until eight in the morning! Stephen sighed and slunk back into the bed, trying to sleep.

Georgia rolled into him and her arm draped over his middle. Before she could trap him, he gently grabbed her wrist and put it on her hip. He looked back at her to make sure she was still asleep. A small mewl escaped her lips. But she settled as Stephen decided to quietly get out of bed.

He carefully walked over to the door, grabbing his pants and hoodie. It was cold out and he didn't want to freeze. Quietly, he opened the door and gently walked down the stairs, not wanting to wake anyone up. When the headlights on the car finally turned off, Stephen was looking at a male figure checking something in the backseat before starting for him. Stephen started for the man, wanting to know who was disturbing the peace here.

When his eyes finally adjusted, he naturally, instinctively went into kill mode.

He growled as he stalked towards Nayla's nephew. He grabbed Jake by the collar of his shirt, ready to deliver the killing blow. But he stopped when a little girl whimpered in the man's arms. Stephen let go and stared at the little girl. She looked so much like her mother, who was back inside sleeping.

Shocked, Stephen glared at Jake, not flattered in the slightest that he had come back.

"She's better off without you," Stephen grumbled.

"Please, tell me she's awake," Jake whispered. "I need to talk to her."

"My daughter's asleep," Stephen snapped "You can talk to her in the morning. Now, leave."

Jake shook his head. "I'm not going to my cabin until Blair can see her," he said.

"I'm not waking her!" Stephen growled in a whisper, getting in Jake's face.

The little girl that he could only assume was his granddaughter, buried her face into Jake's shoulder.

"Take your daughter with you," Stephen ordered. "She can see her mom in the morning."

Jake dropped his voice to a harsh whisper. "But is it true?"

Stephen furrowed his eyebrows in confusion.

"Did she forget about us?"

Stephen nodded his head to confirm Jake's suspicions. "And I'm guessing it has to do with the scar you gave her." He knew of Georgia's scar since she showed it to him.

"I didn't give her anything!" Jake snapped in a whisper, taking his turn to get in Stephen's space. "Not a scratch!"

"Then where did it come from!" Stephen hissed.

"An accident," Jake explained. "Georgia and I got in a fight."

"So, you stabbed her."

"Daddy," Blair said in a cute little voice, making Stephen rethink his approach on the subject.

Jake shook his head in denial. "No. She ran out of the house furious I wouldn't convert. I went after her. But…" Jake's eyes got moist. "A car hit her while she was crossing the road. She had a liver transplant to save her life."

"Who's?" Stephen pressed low.

"A young woman that was her second cousin."

Stephen winced. He got the news. His cousin's daughter passed away in her sleep. She'd sleep apnea that was never properly diagnosed or cared for, and she'd suffocated in her sleep, her mind forgetting to tell her to breathe or wake up.

But Stephen wasn't told by anyone that his cousin's daughter was a donor! He never knew about Georgia's accident! Why wouldn't anyone tell him? He could've brought Georgia home at the first sign of her memory loss! He would have cared for her!

"I went to that funeral," Stephen mumbled. "Why didn't you reach out?"

"I," Jake started, trailing off. "Didn't know you were…in Alabama. I'm sorry."

Stephen growled in frustration, hating the man that took his daughter from him. "Get the fuck outta here." He started back for the door to his trailer.

"Not until we see Georgia," Jake spoke firmly.

Oh, he had nerve. Stephen would give him that, if nothing else.

Stephen stopped in his tracks and looked back at the man that kidnapped his little girl, the man that had made him miss the past five years of her life. He'd been in the dumps, drinking non stop as he missed his family. They never should have gone in the first place. At least Rayleigh's ovarian cancer had been hereditary and bound to happen. Georgia *could've* stayed. But she decided to rebel against Stephen whenever he tried to parent her.

"I'm not waking my angel," Stephen growled threateningly. "But you can be my guest."

Jake shook his head. "Last time I did that was the day we met. And if Avery didn't intervene, we would've conceived then and there."

Truly pissed, Stephen's growl shook his body as he stalked over to Jake and threw a punch into his head. Jake went down, but Stephen grabbed the little girl before she could go down with him. Her little arms wrapped around Stephen's neck and he got protective of his little grandbaby almost instantly. She might just be the only one he'd ever get. Stephen needed to get to know her while he could.

He held her tightly to his side, letting her breathe. He glided over to the trailer and got in. Bears can have Jake. Stephen didn't care. He knew the man was alive, but he was going to be knocked out for quite some time.

"What's your name?" He asked the little girl that he held, softening his voice to something kinder.

"B - Blair," she whispered, staring up at him.

"Well, Miss Blair, you can sleep with momma and I," Stephen whispered to Blair.

She nodded her head. "Are you my pa?" Her southern accent was heavy, showing that she and Jake still lived in Alabama.

After finding out Georgia got Mella's liver, it gave Stephen the closure he needed. Mella had lived in Alabama until the day she died. Stephen bet he could still find his way to her house. He got in the trailer carefully and gently with Blair. He went to the bedroom and did what any father would do for his daughter. He closed the bedroom doors and locked them to give him and Georgia more privacy. Who knew when Jake was going to wake up. But Stephen needed to be prepared just in case Jake tried to get in.

"Mommy," Blair whispered in Stephen's ear. She sounded relieved to see Georgia.

Stephen set Blair on the bed and she crawled over to her mom. He grabbed his gun from the safe, walked out the back door that was connected to the bedroom, then locked it with his key. He was keeping his baby safe from Jake. Jake could throw any kind of accusation he wanted at Stephen. But he wasn't getting to Georgia and convincing her to leave with him. It wasn't going to happen. Stephen walked around the trailer and through the front door of the trailer, locking it behind him.

No one was getting in here as long as he was here. He was making sure his daughter and granddaughter stayed safe. Jake couldn't get to them anytime soon. That was a promise Stephen was making to them. Safety from whatever they need protected from.

*~*~*

Georgia woke up to the sun just barely peeking over the mountains. It had been so cold last night, there had to be dew outside if not frost. She'd frozen alone in the bed, again, until she was wrapped in warmth.

Now, she knew why.

A little one had made their way into the bedroom with Georgia. But she had no idea why Trevor's five-year-old would come into the trailer. Georgia snuggled into Jackie, enjoying the cuddles. She giggled, but it didn't sound like her.

"Mommy, that tickled," the little girl said. That was not Jackie. But the voice… It sounded so familiar.

Georgia's heart screamed for her to remember and she wished she could. Did she have a daughter? Something told her that she did. But she couldn't think of what was speaking to her.

Georgia looked at the little one in her arms and she was thrown into flashbacks. Ones she had no idea she had. The first one came to her like a freight train, its lights shining bright in her mind.

*Georgia was getting woken up.*

*She looked up into the face of the most gorgeous man she'd ever seen. He looked older than her by at least five years. She wanted him. She wanted to take him here and now. Georgia kissed the man. He moaned into her lips, but he didn't push her off. She swiftly grabbed his belt to unbuckle it. It smacked against her hand, but she didn't care. Georgia reached into the man's pants to feel him, eager to lose her virginity. But the door opened and Avery was standing in the doorway with an evil grin.*

Georgia furrowed her brows in confusion. Who was that man? A friend of Avery's? No… her Cousin, maybe?

*Georgia found herself wrapped in the man's embrace, feeling him deep inside of her. Jake… That was his name.*

*His blond hair tickled her cheek, but she didn't care. She was making love to her boyfriend for the very first time and she was enjoying it. It hurt at first, but she was now enjoying every single minute of it. Their breaths mingled, their sweat merged together.*

*Jake took Georgia's hand and entwined his fingers with hers. Standing just a few inches taller than her, she was able to lift her head and kiss him. Their lips fused together and he moaned into her mouth. He growled when she tightened her thighs on his ass. It created vibrations through her, making her go into a beautiful orgasm.*

Georgia couldn't help getting wet as she started to remember this beautiful man. *Jake…* He meant something to her…something so big she couldn't put it into words.. But what was he to her anymore? Without warning Georgia got thrown into another flashback.

*Stephen was furious as Georgia sat in front of him. He was holding a pregnancy test that she'd just taken. He caught her as she waited for the results. They flashed in front of her as he took it. He stared at it with his brows furrowed. Stephen looked at his daughter after a moment.*

"How could you," Stephen breathed, sounding betrayed.

Georgia lifted her chin. "I have my own life to live, Dad."

Stephen shook his head. "Not with Jake, you don't." He grumbled.

"You have no right!" Georgia snapped, standing up.

"We're done with this conversation, Georgia!" Stephen bit back. "You're grounded! For a year!"

Georgia shook her head at her father. "You don't get to parent anymore! You lost that privilege during your first tour!"

Stephen clenched his jaw, a growl escaping his chest.

Georgia gasped from the rage in her dad's eyes as she remembered. But before she could react, she was tossed into another memory.

Georgia snuck out the window with her suitcase full. She wasn't staying here where she would be grounded. She was running away. She already talked to Jake and he was up for it.

*They wanted a life together. And they were getting it.*

*Georgia was marrying this man in this state or another! She didn't exactly know what love was, but she felt as though she had it with her baby's father. She handed the suitcase to him as he stood below her at the back patio, where the lights were out. He quickly took it and set it down. Jake reached for Georgia and she dropped down towards him. He caught her and held her close, his arms tight around her waist.*

*"I got you," he whispered in her ear. "And I always will."*

*Georgia nodded her head, grateful to have a man that loved her so.*

Jake… Sweet Jake. Oh, Georgia loved him sweetly and madly at the same time. But what about Stephen? How did he react when he discovered Georgia ran away? She started to remember everything and decided to reminisce on the good times.

*Georgia was in the delivery room, laughing as she and Jake waited for the doctor to get in. She wasn't dilated, but she was close. Jake grabbed Georgia's bra that she took off to get into the hospital gown and he put her bra on his head. He looked silly. He did a little robot dance, making Georgia giggle.*

*"I am your master," Jake said in a robot voice. He looked at Georgia. "Give me your sanity."*

*Georgia bellowed out a laugh and she felt something slip. She didn't know what it was, but she suddenly felt relief. Jake stared at her exposed crotch in disbelief.*

*"Georgia," Jake whispered. "She's…"*

*The doctor came into the delivery room. He rushed over to Georgia, working at her crotch. She heard a snip. Then a slap. A baby cried and Georgia knew she just delivered without even having to push. She guessed she was dilated while the doctor was out. He did his best to soothe the baby. But when it was time, he handed the little girl to Georgia. Jake joined her side and kissed her head.*

*"She's beautiful, Georgie," Jake whispered.*

*"Blair," Georgia corrected, "her name is Blair."*

Georgia looked at her daughter. Oh, she remembered.

How the sight of Blair made it all come back would be a mystery. But all Georgia could do now was relish in the moment as she continued to have flashbacks.

The fights with Jake. The restless nights with Blair. The love making when it was good between Jake and Georgia. The memories made with such a beautiful little girl. The accident… Georgia cringed as she saw the lights of the caravan in her mind.

She remembered. She knew how she got the scar. A liver transplant. From Mella! Oh, Georgia would always be grateful for her second cousin. But it was sad that Mella had passed away. Georgia and Mella weren't close, but Mella was there for her while she lived in Alabama.

Alabama. Did Georgia dare to go back? Or should she stay here with Blair? Something must've happened to Jake. It had to. Tears burned Georgia's eyes as sadness took over her. She loved him. Truly. Madly. Irrevocably. He was the best thing that ever happened to her.

Georgia took a deep breath. Oh, she would always remember Jake as a good man. Even though she wanted him to convert and he wouldn't. He was still one of the good ones when he wanted to be.

"Mommy, why are you crying?" Blair asked, bringing Georgia out of her trance.

"I missed you," Georgia whispered. "And your daddy."

Blair nodded her head, her dirty blond hair tickling Georgia's cheek. "He's just outside."

Georgia looked up and her eyes clashed with the tan color of the wall. "He is?"

"Yeah."

Georgia instantly got up. She didn't care that she was dressed in just her dad's t-shirt and her panties. She had to see Jake. Was he okay? Why did he leave Blair in here with Georgia? Why didn't he join? Georgia tried to open the doors, not realizing they were locked until she just about broke the lock. She flipped it then bolted out of the trailer, quickly going down the stairs as she barely noticed her dad on the couch, guarding the door as he checked on Blair.

"Don't take too long," Stephen called to Georgia.

"Jake?" Georgia called. She stopped to look around and found Jake lying on the ground. She rushed over to him, knowing what happened. Her dad got to him before anyone else could.

When did he get here?!

"*Jake,*" Georgia got on her knees and took her husband's face in her hands. "Baby, wake up. Jake, come on." She lightly slapped his face, but he didn't wake. She didn't want to slap him hard, afraid that it would piss him off. "Wake up, Jake. Come on, babe."

Someone walked over to Georgia, but she ignored them. "Son of a bitch," Russ spoke up at her back.

"Wake him up, Russ," Georgia begged. Georgia looked up at him. "He's your best friend."

"Not anymore," Russ growled as he shook his head. "He took you from us."

"Newsflash, Russ! I ran away with him!"

Russ winced. He stood there, not moving a muscle.

"Are you gonna get a jug of water or not?" Georgia snapped.

Russ shook his head. Georgia got up, found the cooler of water, took the top off, and carried it over. She splashed the water on Jake, making him sit up instantly. His blue eyes met Georgia's brown eyes after a quiet moment. He got up without a word.

"Blair," Jake mumbled. He started for Stephen's trailer.

"I wouldn't go in there if I were you," Georgia warned. "I didn't see him cause I was too frantic to see you. But I bet he's back on the couch with his gun. He told me not to take too long."

"And you left our daughter in there with him?" Jake snapped threateningly, stalking towards Georgia.

She turned around to face him. "Our daughter is safe with him."

"He's psycho!"

"No." Georgia took a step forward to be even with her beloved husband. At least, she loved him! No one else did! "He's ex-military. Learn the difference."

"Georgia!" Jake snapped. "He has three guns in there!" Jake motioned at the camping trailer next to them, his eyes on Georgia.

"Two." Georgia corrected him. "A handgun and a shotgun."

Jake winced, glaring at Georgia.

"And he'll use any one of them on you." Georgia let her lips brush Jake's lips, knowing she was too close to him for his liking. She couldn't remember why she left, but she had a good idea.

Jake didn't love her anymore. And if that was true, Georgia didn't know how she could change his mind and make him fall in love with her all over again. She sure couldn't get him to go to church with her! She shook her head.

"Don't go in there," she pleaded. "Please."

"Fine," Jake growled after a moment. "But I want my daughter back."

"You gotta be shittin' me."

Jake shook his head. "No."

Georgia sighed in disgust.

"And I honestly don't get that reference," he grumbled "So, I'd appreciate it. If you stopped. Using it!"

Georgia pressed her lips against Jake's. "*Make me,*" she whispered seductively.

Jake thrust his head away, taking a step back. "Bring my daughter-."

"Our," Georgia cut in, "daughter."

Jake looked at Georgia. "Whatever. Bring *our* daughter to the cabin once she's ready. Please." Jake gave his wife an attitude like he always did. She never liked it.

Georgia shook her head. "She's always been a momma's girl. Good luck getting her away from me."

Jake growled threateningly, trying to show dominance. Russ stepped in to show the man who was boss around here, but Georgia grabbed his arm to stop him. Russ squared off with Jake threateningly, making sure he got the message.

It didn't take long before Jake took a step away from the brute and walked over to his car. It must be a rental considering he preferred his truck over anything else. And the license plate had a border around it with some car place title.

"Jake," Georgia spoke up as Jake opened his car door.

He stopped and their eyes met.

"I'm still in love with you." Georgia admitted.

Unfazed, Jake got in his car, started it, and drove out onto the dirt road. He drove away in a cloud of dust, leaving Georgia's heart to break. She sunk down to the ground as she felt it tear, leaving a big hole in her chest. Her family was falling apart. And there was nothing that she could do to fix it.

# Chapter 13

Stephen walked out of the trailer, holding Blair's hand and helping her down. He didn't know Georgia decided to deliver. Let alone keep the baby! She'd cut ties with him and never reached out for the past five years. The moment she left it was as if she dropped off the face of the earth. It tore Stephen and his heart was ripped out of his chest.

He missed his baby. And to find out she had one of her own, he couldn't just let Jake take Blair away. Stephen hoped Georgia would divorce the man. She deserved better. She also deserved her daughter in her life! Stephen wasn't going to let history repeat itself.

"I don't get it," Jessica, Trevor's wife, spoke up, showing her confusion. "Why would he come back?"

Stephen looked over to find Jake gone. Georgia, Russ, Jessica, and Trevor were sitting around the fire pit. Nayla found her way over while Lionel walked over to his truck. Everyone was confused.

"I don't know," Georgia shrugged.

Nayla sat down next to Georgia in the two-person chair. "What happened?"

Georgia looked at Nayla. "Jake," she explained.

Nayla blinked slowly, confused. "You remember?"

"All thanks to seeing my daughter." Georgia looked over at her dad and their eyes met.

He gave her an approving nod, encouraging her to continue. She looked back at Nayla.

"The moment I saw her I remembered," she finished.

Nayla nodded her head.

"Georgie," Stephen started, grabbing his beloved daughter's attention. Their eyes met. He shook his head at her. "Don't let him convince you. Or her. You two deserve better."
"But, Dad," Georgia protested.

"No." He shook his head in disapproval. "I can't afford to lose you a second time."

Georgia sighed and sagged. She nodded her head then turned her attention to Russ as he spoke up.

"Just don't go to his cabin," he said. "I'll take Blair back."

"No!" Georgia jumped up and walked over to Stephen, who handed Blair over to her. She took Blair in her arms then turned to Russ. "You're a stranger to her. My dad or I will take her." Georgia shook her head. "If Jake saw you with Blair, he would freak. And Blair would just panic because she doesn't know you."

Russ sighed in defeat. But he nodded his head to confirm he heard Georgia loud and clear. "Okay. But make it your dad. If Jake so much as lays his hand on you-,"

"He won't." Georgia interrupted. "He won't hurt me. He doesn't have it in him."

"I hope you're right," Russ whispered.

Stephen kissed Georgia's temple. "Let me take Blair to the cabin. You should stay here for the bachelorette party."

Georgia nodded her head then looked up at her dad. "Thanks, Dad," she whispered softly. "I appreciate it."

"Anything for you, baby."

"I'm not your baby," Georgia mumbled.

Stephen met her gaze. "You're my baby girl," he insisted "And my one and only."

Georgia lifted an eyebrow at Stephen, making him realize his words came out wrong. He cringed.

"I mean… You're my one and only daughter," he amended. "And I'm grateful you're my daughter."

"Uh huh," Georgia dragged out teasingly, nodding her head. "I knew you were into incest!"

"Am not!"

"Prove it!"

"Oh, dear," Nayla dragged out, knowing what was about to come.

Georgia got in Stephen's face. "Prove that you couldn't possibly wanna kiss me, Dad."

"Oh, I'll prove a bunch of shit," Stephen teased, nodding his head. "Starting with that birthmark on your ass. Should we see if Blair has it?"

Georgia opened her eyes wide. "You wouldn't," she dragged out.

"Oh, I *so* would."

Georgia blew a raspberry at Stephen, her tongue tickling his lips. If he wasn't against it, he would take his daughter's tongue in his mouth to shut her up. But since he was against incest, he pulled away and rubbed his lips to get rid of her spit. Georgia giggled at him.

"You just rubbed it in," Georgia teased.

"No," Stephen dragged out. "I just wiped it off."

"You enjoy me a little too much," she teased. "Just admit it!" She continued to tease.

Stephen shook his head, refusing to entertain her.

"It's why you suggest I sleep in your bed with you whenever Aunt Colleen and Uncle Rye come up without their trailer!"

"Not true!"

"Alright," Colleen spoke up. "That's it!"

Stephen looked over at his sister as she stood up from her spot. Brown eyes met blue eyes, Colleen's glare piercing Stephen's soul.

"Rye and I are getting our trailer fixed for good. No more of this. Us! Sleeping in your trailer. Georgia is having too much fun with this."

"We both know it's not true, though," Stephen defended himself.

"Of course, not! You would never do that to your own daughter!"

Stephen looked at Georgia with a raised eyebrow. She immediately shut her mouth and pulled back, realizing what she just started. She better be sorry! She just started a riot in front of everyone! Russ started giggling.

"I just wanna say," Trevor started in his teasing, queer voice. "That I love my daughter."

Stephen glared at Trevor, who met his gaze with a teasing one.

"With all my heart."

"Oh, shut up, Trevor!" Stephen groaned. "You all know what I meant!"

Jessica burst out laughing, her round belly protruding from her maternity shirt. "We all know that! We just had to take the chance to tease!"

"Y'all are disgusting," Stephen grumbled.

"Sweet home Alabama," Russ sang as he bounced in his seat with his legs and arms in the air, in a cheerful and teasing mood.

Everybody but Stephen joined in, having fun. He moaned in disgust, turning away. He started for the trailer, but he knew everybody was just going to sing louder for him to hear. He decided to change course and headed for the four-wheeler. As everyone sung their own version of a song about incest in a joking matter, Stephen swung his leg over the four-wheeler, made eye contact with Trevor, and started the vehicle.

"Wait for me," Blair called, clearly wanting a ride.

"Alright," Stephen said. "Be quick and hop on."

Blair hurried over to him as everyone continued to sing in unison somehow. Did they practice together? Did they plan this?! Once sitting in front of Stephen on the four-wheeler, he takes off with Blair without looking back.

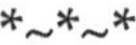

*~*~*

Georgia widened her eyes as Trevor swiftly took his pants off, giving Avery a show. Nayla went bright red, Georgia giggling. She had to laugh.

It may be awkward that Trevor was her cousin, but he was always hilarious with his strip teases. But Georgia knew she could count on Russ to not make it so awkward for her. He always knew how to avert her gaze. Trevor grinded on Avery's lap, making Georgia use her hand to cover her eyes. This was getting way too awkward. But at least Avery enjoyed herself.

"Oh, yes, baby," Trevor teased in his seductive tone. "Touch me."

Georgia got embarrassed, ready to take her daughter and herself to Jake's cabin and ignore everyone's request. She aimed her head low, waiting for Trevor to be done.

"Oh, Russ," Avery moaned teasingly. "Look at you!"

Georgia looked up, just for her eyes to meet her male best friend's. Russ kept eye contact with her as he gave her female best friend a show. He raised his eyebrows at her, giving her an invite. Oh, she could never.

Trevor kept dancing behind Avery, his back pressed into her back. He pushed his butt against her, making her bounce, and arched his back as he came up. Georgia shook her head at her cousin. He did way too well at this; it should be illegal.

Russ took Avery's hands from her sides and laid them flat on his chest. She squealed, laughing as she threw her head back. She was enjoying herself way too much. Her best friend's cousin and best friend, giving her a show of a lifetime. Luckily, Avery wasn't related to either of the men. It was just Georgia.

Georgia looked away, flushed. She didn't know if she could watch her relative and best friend since kindergarten anymore. But she did her best to push through. Suddenly, lips landed near her ear, scaring her. She looked up into twin eyes, Stephen's lips close to hers.

"If you're too embarrassed, then go to the trailer," Stephen mumbled, his voice rumbling through his chest. Oh, it was moments like these Georgia had a crush on her dad. But not a serious one.

It just made her wish she had a man like him. A loving father who would do anything for his little girl and wife. She wanted a male role model for Blair. And if Jake wasn't going to do that with them as a family, Georgia needed to look elsewhere. But would she be able to when she still loved him irrevocably?

"I should probably take Blair to Jake," Georgia muttered.

"I'm coming with," Stephen replied, making Georgia shake her head.

"Please, don't."

"We're going together," he insisted.

Georgia looked over at Avery as her lap dance with both men continued.

"*Now*," Stephen ordered.

Georgia caught Avery's gaze, who gave her a nod of understanding. She got up, taking Blair in her arms from her dad, and followed her dad to the truck. Since Jake didn't leave Blair's booster seat, they had to take Jackie's for the time being. Georgia put Blair in the seat and buckled her up.

"Do I have to go back to Daddy?" Blair asked innocently.

"Of course," Georgia replied sweetly. "But only for a moment. I promise."

"I don't wanna see Daddy."

"Why's that, sweetie?"

"He doesn't love you anymore," Blair whispered.

Georgia's heart sank as she looked at Blair. "And how do you know that?" She suspected as much, but she hated being right. She so hoped this could all turn around!

"He told Uncle Bain."

Georgia put her hand on the toddler seat armrest, her eyes meeting her dad's eyes from the other side. Suspicious, she was sure her daughter overheard the two men. "Oh?"

Blair nodded her head. "I don't want to be with Daddy anymore. I just want to be with you." Her sweet voice made Georgia's heart ache.

"And you will." Georgia looked at Blair. "I promise you, Bee. You won't have to see Daddy unless you want to."

Blair nodded her head, her beautiful blue eyes on Georgia. "Okay. Does that mean we can stay here, then?"

Georgia looked at her dad. "Someone has to go let Daddy know you're not coming. We don't have phone service here."
Stephen nodded his head. "I can go."

"What about the top of the mountain?" Blair insisted.

Georgia looked at her in surprise.

"You and Daddy would always go to the top of the mountain with me whenever we went camping and you needed to call someone," she went on.

Georgia sighed heavily. "Sweetie, I don't think I have your dad's number anymore."

"Please," Blair begged, "try."

Georgia looked up at her dad and he gave her a nod. "Okay," she whispered in defeat. She had to do this. For her daughter.

# Chapter 14

Jake got out of the car and went inside, missing Blair already. He knew he had to drop her off with her mom. She deserved to see Georgia. But Jake didn't want his daughter to be with the woman for very long. Georgia would get convinced to keep Blair! And Jake didn't want that.

He wanted his daughter to stay with him. Accept him. He didn't want her to feel like he didn't love her. He adored his daughter. He would do anything for her. Jake made his way into the cabin. That was when his phone started to ring, showing that it connected to the internet right away.

He looked to see Georgia was calling him. His heart stopped, just for a moment. Did Blair want to come back already? Jake swiped to answer the phone call, putting his phone to his ear.

"She's not coming, Jake," Georgia muttered.

"What do you mean 'she's not coming'?" Jake furrowed his eyebrows, hoping Georgia didn't mean what he thought she meant.

Blair couldn't! She was just four years old! She couldn't betray Jake like that! Yet here he was, finding out his daughter didn't want to come back to him. Crap… What was he going to do?

"I mean," Georgia pressed. "She doesn't want to see you. I'm sorry," she whispered.

"No. Georgia," Jake shook his head in denial.  "You're not sorry."

"Jake," Georgia dragged out, sounding guilt ridden. "You know me."

"That's the problem, Georgia." Jake snapped, opening the fridge as he made it into the kitchen. He grabbed the orange juice. "You've changed. Since the incident. You couldn't get away from Blair and me fast enough."

"I couldn't remember." Georgia's voice squeaked, barely audible. Was she crying?

Jake set the orange juice on the island, realizing what his wife must've gone through. All she had was Avery and Stephen to tell her what happened the past five years. They were both against Jake! Who knew what lies the two were telling Georgia!

"What have they been telling you?" Jake mumbled threateningly.

"I didn't want to hear it from them," Georgia breathed. "I asked them not to say anything about it the six months I've been home."

Jake put Georgia on speaker then put his phone on the counter. He gripped the edges and leaned into it, looking at the device. "Then why the tone of voice, Georgia?"

"Because I miss you," Georgia whispered admittedly.

"No," Jake shook his head. He couldn't believe a word that she said. "No, you don't."

She couldn't do this to him! He was finally moving on and now she's trying to come back?! Georgia. Wasn't. Going. To. Destroy. Jake. Again. She already left when he and Blair weren't home! She must've forgotten to take her medicine!

"Jake," Georgia breathed. "I love you."

"No, you don't," Jake mumbled. He looked at a drawer that was left open and he thrust it closed, pissed off. "Don't tell me something that you think I wanna hear, Georgia!" Jake looked up towards the balcony that led to a few bedrooms upstairs. "I can't afford false hope."

"*Jake.*"

Jake's heart tore at the sound of Georgia's soft voice. She always got this way when they argued and she was crying. Her eyes would always betray her broken heart. It did Jake in every time. He always wanted to make her happy. He sighed, shuddering and closing his eyes.

"Don't," Jake whispered. "Georgia. Just don't."

"I gotta go, Jake," Georgia said on the phone. "My dad needs to go into Bear Lake and

I'm afraid I won't have service for much longer. It's splotchy here."

"Then by all means." Jake looked at his phone. "Go. It's what you do best anyway."

"Oh, fuck you, Jake," Georgia breathed. "I loved you. And I still do. No matter what everybody else says about you… I will always love you."

"And I'll always love my daughter."

"*Our*. Daughter." Georgia whispered.

"Whatever," Jake mumbled. "Bring her back. Please."

"She doesn't want to," Georgia reminded him "She wants to stay with me."

"That is not," Jake started to snap, trailing off. He put his hand over his mouth for a moment before continuing, grasping onto the edge of the island in the middle of the kitchen. "That is not an option," Jake finally said after calming down.

"Then you'll have to come and convince her."

"Maybe I will," Jake muttered. He hung up the phone, unable to listen to Georgia's sweet voice anymore. If he did, he'd fall in love with her all over again. And that was something he couldn't afford to do. He couldn't let Georgia win this war…

Georgia put her hand over her mouth, tears in her eyes. She felt her heart start to tear and it hurt. She hid her face as she rode side by side with her dad. She couldn't let him see her like this. If he did, he'd hurt Jake. Georgia couldn't have that.

As much as she would love Stephen to give Jake a piece of their minds, she knew her dad would go too far. He'd put the man in the hospital if not kill him. And it's just a broken organ. Not a limb.

Georgia sniffed as tears blurred her vision. She didn't notice the great pyrenees chasing after them in Trevor's side by side until it was too late, the dog far behind as it barked.

Stephen's hand landed on Georgia's shoulder, rubbing it lovingly. She tried to ignore him. But he reminded her of how she was once treated by Jake. Foot rubs and shoulder rubs almost every night. Back scratches whenever she couldn't reach an itch. Jake loved Georgia greatly. But now, it was like she was chopped liver. And she hated it. She wanted to be loved, again. Georgia wanted to hear love in Jake's voice whenever they talked. But it was as if it was a chore for him. Did he honestly move on in just six months?!

Georgia shrugged away from Stephen, not wanting his comfort at the moment. He sighed, sounding disappointed, but he didn't say anything. He just continued to drive.

When they finally got to the campsite, Trevor and Jessica were cooking breakfast. Smells of bacon wafted over to Georgia, making her mouth water. But it was hard to think about food when Jake was nearby. When would he come get Blair? Will he come at all? Georgia blindly got out of the side by side just to run into a female body. The woman's arms wrapped around her, the woman's lips so close to her ear.

"I'm so sorry," Avery whispered. "My cousin is an idiot."

Georgia shuddered a sigh. She wrapped her arms around her best friend, grateful that she was still here. She wanted to say something. But she didn't know what to say. Avery rubbed her back.

"Blair deserves you," Avery mumbled. "Don't let Jake try to take her from you. He's selfish."

Georgia shook her head. "She's our daughter."

"And you'll win her in court," Avery insisted.

A small mewl escaped Georgia's lips as she closed them. She didn't want to go to court! She wanted to save her family!

"Think you can eat?" Avery asked softly, knowing her best friend.

"Maybe a couple pieces of bacon," Georgia replied.

Avery nodded her head. "Okay," she whispered.

"Mommy," Blair spoke up from behind Georgia, still sitting in the side by side. "Can I get out, now?"

Georgia pulled away from Avery and started for her beautiful little girl. "Of course, baby." She unbuckled Blair then took her into her arms.

With the helmet on Blair's head, it was a little awkward when she hugged her mom. Georgia felt Avery behind her. A moment later the helmet was taken off Blair's head.

"Oh, my goodness, Blair," Avery breathed enthusiastically. "Look at your hair! It's all staticy!"

Blair giggled as she held onto her mom, her arms draped over Georgia's shoulders. She laid her head on Georgia's shoulder, showing signs that she was already ready for a nap. Serotonin sinking in from the embrace from her daughter, Georgia cherished the moment. Avery cooed at them.

"Georgie, you two are so cute," Avery expressed sweetly. "I just wanna hold her."

Georgia turned around to look at her. "My daughter," she murmured, her eyes drooping as she started to get tired. She couldn't take a nap just yet. She had to eat breakfast first.

"I get to snuggle with her next, then," Avery snorted. "She's my family, too."

Georgia nodded her head, agreeing to let Avery hold Blair even though she was not a baby anymore. She walked over to the double chair and sat down as Blair started to relax into her. Georgia could only imagine how tired Blair must be. She probably slept in the car, but that was never comfortable. Blair must've woken up plenty of times during the night. Especially up this road! For the most part it was smooth, but once you hit a certain point it got rocky. Stephen was always saying he was going to fix it one of these winters.

Georgia laid her head back and let it rest on the chair, sitting low to make it comfortable for Blair. Blair started to snore, her body relaxed into Georgia's. Her little snore lulled Georgia into sleep, though she tried to fight it. Without avail, Georgia fell asleep. But a few minutes later she was woken up with the smell of bacon, cinnamon, and maple syrup. She lifted her head to see a plate of bacon, French toast with maple syrup and powdered sugar, strawberries, and blackberries.

"Thank you," Georgia whispered to Jessica, taking the plate from the pregnant woman.

"You're welcome," Jessica said softly.

Georgia looked up at her.

"Georgia, I wish I knew you five years ago," she continued, sounding sincere. "I honestly think we could've helped each other out. Trevor got me pregnant at that age, but we kept it a secret as long as we could."

Georgia nodded her head as she cut her toast. "You probably would've had some influence on my decision to leave." She looked up at her beloved friend and cousin-in-law.

Jessica nodded her head before walking over to Trevor with her plate of food and sitting with her husband and daughter. Everybody ate, Georgia waking Blair up before she started. Blair woke with a grunt, rubbing her eyes.

"It's okay, baby," Georgia breathed. "I just want you to eat before going back to sleep, okay?" Blair nodded her head as Georgia offered a piece of bacon to her. Georgia shared her food with her daughter, who mainly ate the strawberries and blackberries.

Georgia remembered how much Blair loved her fruit. Watermelon was her all-time favorite, but she was allergic, the food making her face break out in certain spots. The acne was horrible until Georgia figured out her daughter was allergic to the same thing she was. Blair happily ate the other fruit now, not wanting French toast.

Georgia was okay with that, impressed that Blair would eat the bacon. She didn't before. This was a new development. Blair always thought bacon was spicy.

"Is that good?" Georgia asked sweetly.

Blair nodded her head. "It tastes different from the bacon in Alabama."

Realization hit Georgia and she knew what Blair meant. The seasonings. Stephen and Trevor always bought their own pigs at their nearby fair to eat and share with family.

They always seasoned their own meat as well, going with mild seasonings since they had family that couldn't do spicy. Georgia didn't pay much attention when she moved to Alabama with Jake and they bought bacon in the store. But thinking about it, she remembered the bacon tasting a bit different for some reason. It had no seasonings for the most part.

But Georgia started buying bacon that had a couple seasonings when Blair was two years old. She and Jake liked it, but she forgot to think about Blair. If Georgia headed back to Alabama with Jake and Blair, she would have to make sure she went back to buying the other bacon. Feeling like she could sleep all day, Georgia took her last bite of food, finishing off the French toast with two strawberries and eating the last piece of bacon.

"Do you want more?" Georgia asked Blair softly.

Blair nodded her head. "Just one more piece of bacon and then I'm done."

Georgia nodded her head as she finished chewing her food. "Okay. Well, I'm sorry for eating that last piece on the plate."

"It's okay, Mommy," Blair said. "You need your strength."

"Well, so do you."

Blair wrapped her arms around Georgia's neck, giving her a snug hug. "I'm not the one that got hit by a car."

Georgia winced. Luckily, Blair wasn't there when it happened. She was asleep at a friend's house. But Bain and Jake must've talked about it without realizing Blair was in the room.

"I'm okay, sweetie," Georgia breathed. She set her plate down on the ground before stroking Blair's hair to lull her to sleep.

Blair shook her head. "But you're sick, Mommy."

"Oh, no," Georgia whispered. "I'm not sick."

Blair pulled back to look at Georgia, her sweet and beautiful blue eyes on her mom. She held Georgia's face in her hands. "Are you sure?"

Georgia nodded her head, reassuring Blair. "You pwomise?" Blair's sweet little accent slipped through, making Georgia yearn to go back to Alabama one last time.

Would it be different this time?

"I promise," Georgia whispered softly. She kissed Blair's nose before they hugged.

Someone offered Georgia a piece of bacon. She looked up to see it was Stephen. She gladly took it. "Thanks, Dad."

"You're welcome," Stephen mumbled. He walked around Georgia as she offered the piece of bacon to Blair, who gladly took it and gobbled it down. Stephen sat next to Georgia.

But she didn't pay much attention to him as his arm went behind her head on the chair. She was too tired to think about it. Georgia fell back to sleep, glad to have her dad close by.

# Chapter 15

Stephen watched Georgia, worried that she might have it at an earlier age.

This is how it started out. Fatigue.

Georgia usually wasn't one to take a nap after breakfast. Neither was Rayleigh. But it was like someone flipped a switch with Rayleigh, who slept most of the day. This is how it all started out. No… Stephen couldn't lose his little girl.

He was taking her to the doctor the moment they got home from their camping trip. He wasn't letting history repeat itself. It was a priority. Georgia was a priority. She always would be. Georgia shifted in her sleep, mewling as if she was having a bad dream.

Stephen rubbed her thigh comfortingly. After a few minutes of rubbing she settled, sighing heavily. Restlessness. It was already settling in after Georgia had only had Blair for a few hours. Jake's truck pulled up next to Stephen's camp trailer. What was he doing here?

Georgia told him Blair didn't want to go back to him! Trevor pulled up in his truck, the butt of his fishing pole sticking out of the bed. Did he catch anything? Trevor quickly got out, stalking towards Jake as he got out of his truck. Stephen stood up, but he didn't stop Trevor as his nephew stalked over and grabbed Jake by the shirt. He roughly threw the man into his truck, making Jake look puny against him. Trevor was so much of a brawny mountain man he looked like a bodybuilder.

"What the hell is wrong with you?" Trevor spat in a low tone. "Coming back here like you didn't kidnap my cousin."

"She came with me," Jake corrected Trevor, getting a growl from the muscled man.

"Trevor," Stephen spoke low, grabbing Trevor's attention.

Trevor looked over at him. He shook his head, telling his nephew to back down. Trevor begrudgingly let Jake go, taking a step back. Jake kept his eyes on Trevor for a moment before looking over at Georgia. He started for her. But Stephen got in the way.

"What do you think you're doing?" Stephen threatened in a low tone.

Jake met his gaze. "Taking my daughter."

Stephen shook his head. "Blair's not being forced into anything."

"She's coming home with me," Jake insisted.

"She's staying with her mother," Stephen snapped. "You can forget it."

"No," Jake shook his head. "She's my daughter, too."

"I don't give a fuck," Stephen got in Jake's face threateningly. "Now, leave."

Jake shook his head at Stephen, holding his glare. "Not without my daughter," Jake mumbled.

Stephen growled in annoyance, ready to knock the man out, again. But he restrained himself. Pulling back Stephen gave Jake some space. Georgia may have confessed she willingly ran away with him, but he still got her pregnant. Stephen could still hold that against him.

"Georgia didn't ask to get pregnant," Stephen grumbled. "But since she did, her daughter is my granddaughter. And I get to call the shots around here."

Jake glared at Stephen with his lips parted.

"You better run while you still can."

"No." Georgia whimpered from behind Stephen. She mewled, tossing in her chair.

"Stephen, she's having a nightmare," Nayla spoke up.

Stephen backed away from Jake, knowing what calmed his daughter whenever she had a nightmare.

"Dad," Georgia whispered. "Don't hurt him." She pleaded. It sounded as if she somehow knew what was going on around her. But whoever did when they were asleep?

Stephen walked over to her and bent down to look at her. He rubbed her knee. "Baby, it's just a dream," he mumbled.

Georgia panted, terrified. But when Blair shifted, she calmed down. Stephen decided to apply more pressure on his daughter, knowing that was what she needed. He pressed his hand on her chest, above her heart. Knowing this would do the trick, Stephen watched and waited. Georgia slowly opened her eyes.

That was when Jake was taking Blair from her. Blair screamed as she woke up and became frantic. Georgia jumped up to grab her, taking her from Jake. Trevor rushed out of his trailer with a filet knife, Jessica ran past him, but Lionel stalked out of his trailer. He cocked his shotgun and pointed it at Jake. Russ jumped out of his hammock, phone in hand. Stephen put his hand up, letting Lionel know it was nothing serious. He could put his gun down. But Lionel kept it up, threatening his nephew.

"Leave," Lionel ordered in a growl. "And don't come back."

"But, Lionel," Jake defended himself. "You have to understand."

"Oh, I understand plenty," Lionel said. "She was fifteen. You were twenty."

"Lionel, I…"

"I should take you into the station!" Lionel barked. "Now, that you're back!"

"Hold on," Jake pleaded, holding up his hands.

"Give me one reason to," Lionel growled, getting protective of the woman that he helped raise.

Stephen watched Jake, who looked between Lionel and Georgia. Blair cried into her neck, sounding scared. She must get scared easily. This was just a misunderstanding. Stephen knew it. Jake's eyes landed on Georgia, past Stephen's shoulder.

"I just want my daughter," Jake breathed. "That's all I want."

"But she doesn't want to go with you," Georgia mumbled. "She said so herself."

"Blair…" Jake begged, "you can't honestly…"

Stephen looked back at his daughter and granddaughter, who clung onto each other as if life depended on it. Blair looked at her dad after a moment.

"You know you can't pick me up like that," Blair said innocently. "It scares me."

"Wait," Lionel spoke up. "She just… Got startled?"

Stephen looked at his best friend's husband. He nodded slowly. "No need for weapons."

"Well, that's no fun," Trevor spoke up. "I was so hoping for blood."

Stephen glared at his nephew.

"I could use a good time," Trevor went on, shrugging.

"Oh, grow up!" Stephen snapped.

Trevor looked at Stephen, his brown eyes dancing with laughter. That was when Stephen pieced it together. Trevor was just joking.

"Go filet your fish." Stephen ordered.

"With pleasure," Trevor said in a cute voice, turning towards his trailer. "Daddy."

"I'm gonna tell your mother you said that," Stephen warned.

Trevor laughed before heading into his trailer. Stephen looked at Georgia.

"Is she okay?" he asked gently.

Georgia nodded her head. "Yeah," she whispered.

Stephen nodded his head before he looked at Jake, who looked between Lionel and Georgia. "You need to leave," he ordered.

Jake looked at Stephen, blue eyes meeting brown. "No. Not without Blair."

"Lionel, take 'im in," Georgia put in. "You know he had sex with a minor."

Jake glared at Georgia. "I'm not the one that seduced the other!"

"Well, I'm not the one that trespassed on Lechar's property and stole his prized cow!"

"Borrowed!"

Stephen glared at Jake, who pointed at Georgia.

"And he dared me to break in the first place!"

"Well, it's no different," Georgia put in.

Lionel pulled his handcuffs out and started for Jake.

"What about that time you tipped Lechar's prized cow into that ditch?" Jake challenged.

Stephen snorted. He remembered that! Georgia was in so much trouble when Lechar caught her! Lionel started for Georgia, but stopped when he remembered she already did time for that. Twenty hours, equivalent to the time she would've spent in jail. Stephen looked between the bickering couple as they continued to rat the other one out to go to jail. Georgia put her free hand on her hip as she continued.

"What about the skunk you put in daddy's truck?" Her southern accent started coming out and it made Stephen proud.

Jake shook his head. "That's nothing compared to the dead one you put in Lionel's lunch bag!"

Lionel snapped a shocked look at Georgia. "That was you?"

Georgia nodded her head at him. She looked at Jake, her brown eyes daring. "I'm not the one that streaked across the high school football field with his two buddies. Rocko and Richie." Georgia tilted her head to the side, giving attitude. "How are they doing, by the way?"

Lionel started for Jake, who stuttered for a moment.

"Wait!" Jake snapped his fingers as it came together in his head. He pointed at Georgia. "I remember. What about that time you painted the rival high school's mascot in paint that wasn't washable? And you broke the hoof when you wanted to chisel a little piece off."

Lionel growled, stalking towards Georgia. It seemed someone wanted her in jail! Stephen rushed over to stop Lionel, standing in front of his daughter and protecting her. Brown eyes met blue eyes.

"Lionel," Stephen dragged out.

"Stephen," Lionel replied. "Mind if I take your daughter in?"

"I do, actually."

"She committed a crime," Lionel said.

"Which I believe all charges were dropped," Stephen reminded him. "She did time at work. My. Work."

"Stephen, this isn't like those other times," Lionel grumbled.

"I agree." Stephen sighed as he put his hands in his front pockets, keeping eye contact with the police chief. "But we both know boot camp is worse than jail." He leaned in. "And that's exactly what she got." Stephen held eye contact with Lionel for a few good minutes before the sheriff finally caved in.

He put his cuffs back in his belt, keeping eye contact with Stephen. Lionel sighed. "She's forgiven," he mumbled.

Stephen nodded his head. "Thank you."

Lionel offered his hand to Stephen and he took it in a firm shake. "You're welcome." Lionel put his lips near Stephen's ear. "In all honesty, I had a feeling it was her."

"So, did I," Stephen whispered in Lionel's ear.

They nodded their heads as Stephen slipped bail money for Georgia into Lionel's hand. Lionel backed up.

"That's it?" Jake asked in disbelief.

Lionel looked at his nephew. "That's it." He held the money up. "Bail money."

"Bullshit," Jake cussed.

"I agree. But Stephen had it." Lionel looked at Stephen and winked at him. They both knew where the money was going to go once it was given to the station. The mancave the station has been working on.

Stephen watched Jake as he took something out of his rental car and started for Georgia. Stephen caught a file in Jake's hand, making him wonder what it was. Did Jake and Georgia get married? When would they have done that? Georgia met Jake's gaze as he approached her and handed her the file.

"Papers," Jake mumbled. "Sign 'em."

Georgia shook her head, tears in her eyes. "No," she whispered.

"Damn it, Georgia!" Jake snapped. "Just sign them!"

"I'm still in love with you, Jake." Georgia defended herself. She looked broken. Ready to break down.

Jake's gaze faltered for a moment. But he looked Georgia right in the eyes once he was able to look at her. "Yeah, well. I'm not." He looked at Blair, her bright blue eyes moist. "I'm sorry, Blair," he whispered.

"No!" Blair screamed. She buried her face into Georgia's neck as Georgia stared Jake in the face, her heart clearly breaking.

Stephen's heart broke with hers, wanting her to be happy.
"I want a divorce," Jake grumbled.

Tears escaped Georgia's eyes as Blair cried into her neck.

# Chapter 16

Jake shifted, uncomfortable about staying at Stephen's property. He knew he was unwelcome, but he had to take Blair back. He wasn't letting her stay with Georgia. They needed to go home. Back to Alabama. But Blair won't let Jake near her. Every time he tried to get close… She would scream and cry for Georgia.

Jake couldn't have that. It broke his heart, making him wish he could mend little Blair's heart. Stephen had his stethoscope on, listening to Georgia's ovaries. If that was really a thing… Was something wrong?

Jake lifted his chin, watching father and daughter as they conversed sweetly. It seemed like forever since the two of them got along. Stephen was always grounding Georgia over something when she was just a teenager. Jake remembered a time Georgia pranked her nemesis! She got in trouble for it. Jake's heart yearned for Blair to look at him the way Georgia was looking at Stephen. Love and admiration showed in her eyes, her face soft.

Jake sighed and sagged, missing how it used to be just a few days ago. Blair ran for the ball that her second cousin threw to her. The ball made its way towards Jake. He stopped it with his foot and bent down to grab it. Blair stopped to stare at him. Jake held the ball out to her with a soft smile on his face.

"Come on, Blair," Jake breathed. "You know I'd never hurt you."

"But you did," Blair spoke up, her sweet voice thick with her southern accent.

"I didn't mean to, sweetie." Jake shook his head. "You know I love you."

"Then why can't you love Mommy?" Blair begged.

Jake shuddered a sigh. "Because Mommy doesn't need me. She's got pa."

"But she said it herself!" Blair yelled. "She loves you!"

Jake shook his head. "It's a little too late for me, sweetie," he whispered.

Blair walked over to Jake, letting him believe he was making progress. But she snatched the ball from his hands with a "hm", glaring at him. She walked away with the blue dodgeball, her hands looking smaller than normal against it.

"Dad, I'm fine," Georgia squeaked.

"Just let me check," Stephen defended himself.

Jake looked over at the bickering father and daughter.

"My butt isn't my ovaries!" Georgia yelled. She struggled against Stephen as he pinned her to the chair. "Nayla!" She reached out to Jake's aunt as she walked by. "Save me!"

Nayla stopped to look at the situation. "Oh, no," she dragged out, holding her mug of tea. "I get involved and your father won't let it go for years."

"But…"

"Sorry, sweetie," Nayla sighed. "You're on your own."

"Russ!" Georgia screamed as Stephen flipped her on her stomach, across the two-person chair.

He put his stethoscope to her kidneys. She picked her head up in realization.

"Oh, wait."

Stephen smacked Georgia's ass once he had a good listen, getting a scream out of her. "That's for fighting with me." He got up and walked away, seeming to be satisfied for the moment. But when Jake caught the look on Stephen's face, he knew there was something wrong.

Jake started for Stephen, needing to know what was wrong. If Georgia was sick, Jake had to make sure Blair got all the time she needed with her mom. Avery, Jake's cousin, stepped in front of him, making him nearly collide with her.

"Jake," Avery dragged out.

Jake took a step back, looking at her. "Avery."

"You really shouldn't have come back," she said.

"Blair wanted to see her," he explained. "And I had papers to deliver."

"You could've sent them in the mail, let Georgia believe that she didn't love you and that it was why she left."

Jake shook his head. "Not my fault she remembered." He walked past Avery, setting their conversation aside.

"Wha," Avery trailed off. "Jake!"

Jake caught Stephen at his truck. He grabbed his shoulder gently, letting him know he was there in a friendly manner. Blue eyes met brown eyes.

"What's going on," Jake mumbled.

"None of your concern," Stephen muttered.

"Hey." Jake snapped, stopping Stephen from walking away. "Georgia's my baby mama. If she's sick, I need to know how much time Blair has with her!"

"Like I said," Stephen grumbled. "None of your concern. It's just mine and Blair's alone."

Jake winced. Ovarian cancer. Rayleigh had it. Jake knew it was genetic considering Rayleigh's mom died from it. They never caught it in time.

Stephen left Jake alone, stopping when he saw Avery. He shook his head, letting Jake know the man was in love with his cousin. Great… If Stephen won Avery's heart, he'd be Jake's cousin-in-law! He couldn't have that! The man hated him as it is! How could Jake convince Avery not to love the man back? Was there anything he could hold against him?

Avery stepped into Georgia and Blair looked up at them. She didn't know what they were talking about, but she knew it was something serious. Their body language said it all. Jackie ran over to Blair and took the ball.

"Come on," Jackie whispered excitedly. "My dad has a game we can play."

Blair followed Jackie, catching a few words from her mom.

"I can't believe he'd do this to Blair," Georgia whispered.

Blair stopped to listen, curious to know what her mom was talking about. She tilted her head to the side. What was her mom saying?

"I love my little girl. Truly. And I wouldn't have remembered if it wasn't for her," Georgia went on. "But why bring her in the first place?"

Avery sighed heavily. "Maybe he does have a heart," she mumbled. "And he decided to let Blair see you, once again."

Georgia shook her head. "He's always had a heart," she mumbled. "He just doesn't like to show it."

Avery snorted.

Jackie ran over to Blair and grabbed her by the arm as Blair thought about her mom's words. Was it true? Could her dad have done this for her? If so, she wanted to thank him. But she still had a hard time with her dad lying to her. He told her something different in Alabama. But once they came to this Utah place…

He was different. And Blair didn't like it. She didn't know what was wrong with her dad. But if he was going to be like this, she didn't want to be with him. Blair hoped her daddy loved her mommy. She wanted them together. They were happy together no matter what they went through.

Blair would never know what happened to her mommy, why Georgia was so different suddenly. But Jake seemed to be even worse. Blair just knew Georgia loved her. And she knew her mom would do anything for her. Georgia was a good person and Blair was always attached to her because of that.

Blair followed Jackie into her daddy's trailer, where they were greeted by a huge dog! It sniffed both of them before giving them a kiss in turn. Blair giggled at the tickling sensation. Oh, she missed Waldo. He was a good dog. Back in Alabama he was being watched by uncle Bain's parents.

"Willie," Trevor snapped. "Leave them alone." He ordered his dog.

Blair didn't mind. She hugged the Irish wolfhound's neck, standing shorter than the massive dog. He took up the whole trailer! What was he doing in here?

"I'm sorry, Blair," Trevor started. "He wouldn't hurt a fly. But he's a slob."

"I like him," Blair replied. "Don't be sorry."

"Do you have a dog?"

Blair nodded her head, looking up at her mommy's cousin.

"What breed is he?"

"Bloodhound."

"Oh," Trevor dragged out, a smile on his face. "Those are so cute."

Blair nodded her head.

"What's his name?"

"Waldo."

"Oh, my goodness! I'm gonna have to meet him."

Blair got excited at the news of having family come visit. "I would love that!"

Trevor nodded his head. "I got a game for you two. Think you can do it?"

"Depends on the game." Blair clasped her hands in front of her and swung her hips side to side. She liked Trevor. He was super cute with his beard and short brown hair. Mommy would call him a mountain man. But he looked like an MMA fighter to Blair. Trevor leaned down to Blair's eye level.

"A race," Trevor breathed in a tease. "We're gonna see who can annoy your dad the most the fastest."

Blair nodded her head, a smile on her face. She was good at that. Annoying her daddy was easy for her! This would be a piece of cake. She knew it.

# Chapter 17

Georgia got up after finishing her drink. She was trying to stay awake. But she wanted so much to take another nap. She didn't know if it was because of stress about Jake being here. But she did know she missed him.

Oh, she wished he would love her like he did once before. But something changed. She had no idea what, but she would like to know. Georgia still wanted to be with Jake. No matter what it cost.

She yawned, ready for a nap. Someone walked up next to Georgia, his arm sneaking around her.

"Hey," Russ whispered.

"What?" Georgia whispered back.

"How you feeling?"

"Tired," she sighed. "I could use a nap."

"My tent's available so we could. You know."

Georgia looked up at Russ.

"Give him the idea," he said, wiggling his eyebrows.

"Russ, you're nasty," Georgia dragged out softly.

Russ shrugged. "Well, you know how it is."

Georgia shook her head. "This isn't like Avery, you know."

"Oh, she and I had fun teasing Ashton."

"He flipped out!" Georgia spoke up. "The way you two just sauntered over to the bathroom like that?"

Russ laughed. "Bear Lake is the place to be."

"And the incident stays there."

Russ snorted. He smiled, making Georgia smile with how infectious his brightness was. Georgia giggled as she remembered the aftermath.

"Jake walked in on you two, didn't he?" Georgia reminisced.

"Almost," Russ shook his head. "We opened the door before he did."

Georgia snorted, leaning into her dad's trailer and looking up at Russ. "That was hilarious."

Russ nodded his head, a bright smile on his face. "Oh, I totally agree."

Georgia leaned towards Russ. "If you kissed me to try and make Jake jealous, I wouldn't be opposed," she muttered.

Giving into the idea, he went for it. He wrapped his arm around Georgia's waist then dipped her, putting his lips on her neck. She widened her eyes.

"Oh," she said out loud, not knowing how to act in this situation.

Russ nipped Georgia in the neck. His lips trailed up to her jaw, kissing it. His lips teased her skin as they went to her ear, making her flush. She didn't know he was this seductive!

"This is exactly what I did to Avery," Russ whispered in Georgia's ear. "To make her flush."

"*Oh*," Georgia moaned as Russ sucked on her earlobe.

It's a wonder why he was suddenly single! He wasn't quite gay no matter how well he pulled it off. Could he maybe be bisexual? It would explain a lot!

Georgia went bright red as Russ held her thigh against his hip. He didn't grind against her, but she could tell he was turned on. That's when she figured it out. Russ was in love with her.

No wonder he looked heartbroken when she confessed she liked his brother! He was hoping she liked him! Georgia's heart broke for Russ, wishing she could see him as more than a friend. It would fix a lot of things for all of them.

But Georgia didn't know if this would make a difference for her opinion about her male best friend. Oh, she hoped he was just doing this to help her get a reaction from Jake! As if it worked, Georgia heard a growl from behind Russ. But when they looked up it wasn't Jake. It was Stephen.

"Dad," Georgia spoke up.

Russ let her back up and turned to face the consequences. Georgia stood next to him.

"I know what you two are doing," Stephen muttered. "And I hate to mention it, but I apologize to say it isn't working. You had me fooled for a moment there, though."

"Is that," Russ dragged out slowly. "A good thing?"

Stephen smiled brightly. "Do it, again. You had everyone looking over here."

"So, that growl…" Russ pointed at Stephen.

"Was just to get your attention. But I know how my daughter thinks of you." Stephen shook his head. "I'm sorry, Russ. But you'll always just be her best friend."

Russ nodded his head then looked at Georgia. Their eyes met.

"I'm sorry," Georgia whispered. "I had no idea until now."

Russ nodded his head, his eyes soft. "It's okay," he mumbled. "You're not the only one I'm in love with."

Georgia nodded her head. "There's someone else?"

"Yeah," Russ reassured her with a brief nod. "Don't worry about it."

"Okay," Georgia whispered. She rubbed Russ's arm before giving him a hug.

His arms wrapped around her. Her chin settled on his shoulder, her eyes meeting Jake's. His blue eyes shone in victory in the sunlight. If he was watching the whole thing… Did that mean he cared? Or was the victory for another reason?

*~*~*

Russ pulled Avery to the side before she could leave with Ashton, wanting to talk to her about Georgia. He knew something was wrong. Georgia never took naps during the day! Was she sick? Or stressed? Would Avery know anything about it?

"What's going on?" Avery mumbled as she and Russ stood half a mile away from the campground.

"It's Georgia," Russ muttered. "She's super tired all of a sudden."

"I know."

"Do you know anything about that?" Russ pressed.

Avery shook her head. "All I can think of is her mom."

Russ shook his head, realization hitting him. "No… You don't think…"

Avery nodded her head in confirmation. "It's sooner than Rayleigh. But if it's true…"

"Georgia only has a few more months."

"Poor Blair," Avery sighed. "She's going to grow up without a mom."

"Is there any cure at all?" Russ pressed, wanting to save his best friend.

She deserved to watch her daughter grow up. She deserved to stay here healthy! Avery's eyes filled with tears.

"If it's advanced as much as Rayleigh's before it was caught," Avery murmured. "I'm afraid not."

Russ shook his head. "Please, no. I can't lose her."

"Neither can I, Russ." Avery moved in and hugged him tightly. "Neither can I."

Tears filled his eyes as he clung onto his other best friend.

"I'm sorry, Russ," Avery whispered. "I know how much you love her." She rubbed Russ's back comfortingly.

"I hope we're wrong," Russ muttered. "I hope that she's just stressed."

"I saw the look on Stephen's face after he listened to Georgia's ovaries," Avery whispered.

"But you can't hear cysts!" Russ snapped. "Or tumors!"

"But you can hear an abnormality," Avery said. "Maybe that's what Stephen heard."

Russ shook his head. "Not possible," he breathed, his voice barely a whisper.

Avery shook her head, clearly in denial as much as Russ. "I don't want it to be either," she whispered.

Russ shuddered, doing his best to keep his tears in. He held onto Avery. When she gave him a tighter squeeze of reassurance, the tears came down. And they wouldn't stop.

# Chapter 18

Ashton watched Stephen as their eyes met, his eyes in a glare. Stephen shook his head at the young man, unable to socialize with him. Ashton still had a lot to learn.

Stephen may have deserved the wake-up call from the engaged man, a punch square in the jaw. But it didn't mean he had to talk with him. Stephen walked over to Georgia, who was pulling food out of the cooler for lunch. He rubbed her shoulder blades lovingly as she stood up straight, opening a package of bacon.

"How you feeling?" Stephen asked.

Georgia used her pocket knife to open the bacon after failing with just her hands. "Fine," she mumbled. She looked up at her dad. "Why?"

"I'm just worried."

"About what?"

"Everything sounded fine, but… I'm not convinced."

Georgia sighed and sagged. "You think I have ovarian cancer."

"Sweetie, your mom and grandma had it," he reminded her. "It's hereditary."

Georgia nodded her head, considering her options. She looked ready to take another nap, but Stephen hoped he was wrong. "I wanna get tested, then."

Stephen nodded his head. "Okay," he whispered, proud of his daughter for making the right decision. "I'm proud of you, Georgie."

Georgia fought back a smile, but she failed. "Thanks, Dad," she whispered.

Stephen grabbed the onion and the sliced cheese from the cooler. "Let me help cook."

Georgia nodded her head. She led Stephen over to their cooker. She laid bacon in the dutch oven pot, which was already on and heated up. She must've turned it on without Stephen knowing. He set the onion and cheese on the table then grabbed a knife to slice the red onion.

Jessica sliced tomatoes on the other end of the table, her belly protruding from her maternity shirt. Stephen glanced over at her before continuing to slice.

"How's momma feeling?" Stephen asked his niece-in-law.

She nodded her head in his peripheral vision. "I'm ready to give birth. This baby keeps pushing on my bladder."

Stephen laughed, a smile on his face. "I'm surprised you agreed to come up."

"It's Avery," Jessica said. "She's a good friend of mine."

"What did you think of your husband giving her a lap dance a couple days ago?"

Jessica snorted, pressing her lips together. "It was hilarious. And it reminded me why I love him so much."

Stephen looked at her. "Don't tell me he gives you shows."

Jessica nodded her head. "He does, actually. And sometimes it's hilarious."

Stephen shook his head as he got back to cutting the onion. "I never would've thought Trevor would do something like that."

"We keep it a secret."

Stephen snorted. He could see why!

Trevor usually came off as a serious mountain man, hiking, hunting, and fishing. He went shed hunting when it was the season after deer and elk shed their antlers. Trevor always drew a tag for a deer and an elk every year, very much into outdoor activities. He wasn't one to stay indoors. And he also worked out a little. His dad was a bodybuilder and invited him to go to the gym with him. Trevor never passed up the opportunity to take care of himself in every way. He went to school to be a personal trainer, but then he decided to turn around and go to school for wildlife conservation.

"My lips are sealed," Stephen finally spoke up, a small smile on his face.

"Don't tell him I told you," Jessica whispered teasingly.

"Oh, I wouldn't dare," Stephen mumbled.

*~*~*

Blair kicked the ball towards Jake, who caught it before it could hit him. He looked over at her, noticing how she slumped in disappointment. Oh… She's going to try to annoy him! That little brat sure knew how to push Jake's buttons sometimes. He still loved her, though. He dropped the ball but then thought better of it.

He picked it up as Georgia called for lunch. Her loud whistle called everyone's attention, her fingers in her mouth to press her tongue down. She was good at that. She was unique in many ways, her whistling technique one of them. It's what made Jake fall in love with her in the first place. He didn't know if lunch was for him, deciding to stay back. When Georgia looked at him their eyes met.

"You, too," Georgia spoke up. "Dingbat. Come get a sandwich."

Jake nodded his head. He wanted to leave. Take Blair home. But Georgia hadn't signed the papers yet. When would she do that? Jake would like to get the divorce started and done as quickly as possible. He waited until everyone came and got their sandwich, not wanting to step on any toes.

Trevor was the first one, grabbing three sandwiches. He gave one to his wife, who Jake had no idea was. Trevor handed the smallest sandwich to his little one, grabbing her attention while she played with Blair. Trevor's little one took the sandwich and happily ate it, making a small growl of approval.

"I love mustard!" Trevor's little one cried out.

Jake snorted as everyone laughed, smiles on their faces. Jake couldn't smile. Not here. It was too hostile for him to feel like smiling. Jake felt eyes on him. Catching Georgia looking at him, he quickly looked away. He couldn't look at her. Not now.

What if she pulled him in? Would he forgive her for running away? He didn't care that she couldn't remember! She ran from their daughter! Who could do such a thing?!

The smell of onion hit Jake's nose strongly. Knowing a sandwich was underneath it he dared to look at it, his mouth salivating.

"Eat," Georgia mumbled.

He should've known. Jake growled, unwilling to take a sandwich from his wife. He leaned into his rental car, away from the sandwich.

"I didn't poison it, Jake," Georgia snapped, glaring at Jake. "Now, eat!"

"I'd rather a gator take my arm than take one of your offerings," Jake mumbled.

"Oh, grow. Up!"

Jake shook his head at Georgia, dismissing her as he looked up over the car to look at the railing on top of it.

"We have a daughter together!" She went on, yelling. "And if you're acting like this around her, I don't blame her for wanting to leave you!"

Jake snapped a glare at Georgia. "You listen to me. Georgia-,"

She shook her head, cutting him off. Tears filled her eyes and he knew it wasn't because of the onion. "*No*. I'm done listening to your lame excuses." Georgia leaned in towards Jake as he turned to face her. "I love you, Jake. I'm still in love with you. But you always had the worst excuses for not going to church with Blair and I," she snapped.

"I wasn't of the religion, Georgia!"

Georgia winced, pulling her head back.

"How could I go?!" He raged on. "It wasn't the place for me at the time!"

"So, you've changed."

Jake winced, realizing what he just confessed. He took a moment, thinking about the past six months. Yes. He's changed. He started going to church, hoping Georgia would come home. But after a few months, Jake gave up on her.

"Yes," Jake whispered. He cleared his throat, looking to his side. He took a step back. "Yeah." Jake finally met Georgia's gaze. "I started going."

Georgia scoffed in disbelief. She shook her head at Jake. "Who?"

Jake narrowed his eyes. "What?"

"Who convinced you to go?"

Jake shook his head at Georgia. "No one."

"Bullshit… Tell me what," Georgia snapped. "Woman! Got you to go!"

"If we're going to be technical-."

"Yes!" Georgia interrupted Jake. "Jake! I want you to tell me the truth! Who got you to go to church?! After all this time-."

"*You*!" Jake snapped, cutting Georgia off.

She stopped mid-sentence, wincing at Jake.

"Georgia, it was you!" He repeated. "It was always you! I loved you!"

Georgia took a step back, showing signs she was getting scared. Jake knew to back down when she got this way. She was frightened, fearful of her life. She should know he would never hurt her! Not in a million years! Not in this life! Nor the next! Jake got in Georgia's space anyway, wanting to get his point across. He shook his head at her.

"There was a time," Jake breathed, not wanting anyone to hear his conversation with his wife he once loved. "I would've done anything to get you back. To make you remember."

Georgia shook her head at Jake, wide-eyed.

"I wanted us," Jake hissed, "to be a family, again! I didn't want you to leave the house! I never wanted you to run! I wanted to help you remember." Emotions flooded Jake as he remembered the night he and Georgia got in that fight.

*They were arguing. Fighting! About the same damn thing! It was the only thing they ever fought about! Georgia wanted Jake to go to church with her! And now Blair!*

*Ever since Blair was born the fights got worse every time. Jake never hit Georgia. She never hit him. But they would put holes in the walls, knock chairs and tables over, and have mad make-up sex after. But this time… It was different. As if Jake knew what was about to happen next, he grabbed Georgia's arm to keep her from storming out the door that would lead her to her fate. But she slipped away from him anyway, having enough.*

*"Georgia!" Jake called as he followed his beloved wife out.*

*She went straight to the road. Jake looked over as he heard a car screech, coming around the bend way too fast. It was drunk Leo, again. Fear struck Jake as he looked over at the love of his life. The one woman he could never lose.*

*"Georgia!" Jake screamed, watching as the lights bore down on her. "No!"*

*Tires screeched, a thump was heard, then everything went dark.*

Jake shook his head as he shuddered. The flashback… It hurt way too much. How was he going to continue this conversation from here?

"Do you remember it at all?" Jake whispered. "The… Accident?"

Georgia shook her head. "I remember the fight," she mumbled. "The same damn one we had every week."

"But Leo?"

"No." Georgia pulled away from Jake as he towered over her. She was five feet and five inches. Jake was six feet and one inch. It only ever bothered her when he got in her face like this.

He shuddered a sigh. "I want a divorce, Georgia."

"Yeah, well, I don't," Georgia mumbled. She shoved the sandwich into Jake's chest and he caught it. "Eat it. I know you're hungry." Georgia turned around, leaving Jake behind.

At her leave, Jake took that as a sign to go. If he stayed any longer, Lionel would put a bullet in his head. Jake got in the car, knowing Blair didn't want to see him. He would try, again. But he already pushed it earlier. He had to leave for just a little bit.

# Chapter 19

Georgia stared at the ground, her feet on the chair. With her knees curled in towards her chest, she stared off into space. She wished Jake still loved her. He'd changed for her!

Now, six months after the "incident" Georgia didn't remember, he wanted nothing to do with her. What changed? What made Jake decide Georgia wasn't worth it anymore?

It better not be Blakely! That woman is a good woman. But Jake always pined after her after they met. Georgia tried not to let it get to her. But deep down it did. She wanted to get Jake away from Blakely by having him go to church with her. It was always Sundays when Blakely would come by to keep Jake company while Georgia was at church. Who knew what they did behind Georgia's back!

Blair got on the chair to hug her mom's neck, interrupting her thoughts.

"Mommy," Blair asked.

"Hmm," Georgia replied questioningly.

"Why is daddy so mean when we're here?"

Georgia sighed and sagged. "Everyone thinks he kidnapped me when we were younger."

"Did he?"

Georgia shook her head. She looked at her beloved daughter. "No. He would never do anything of the sort."

Blair's blue eyes shone bright in the sun. Her brown hair was so light it was almost a dirty blond in the sun.

"Your daddy and I loved each other once," Georgia mumbled to Blair. "Back before you were born. We lived here. We met and we fell in love. We got to know each other. I know your daddy. He would never hurt me."

"But he did."

"Blair." Georgia dragged out, trying to reassure her daughter.

"He broke your heart. And mine. I don't think I could forgive him. I don't think I could forget it," Blair whispered, looking down. On her knees next to Georgia, she sat there, looking like she was contemplating life already at such a young age.

"He loves you, Blair," Georgia spoke up. She lifted her beloved daughter's chin. Brown eyes met blue eyes. She shook her head. "He would never hurt you, Blair."

"But he did, Mommy," Blair insisted. "He said he lied to me. Back home he said he loved you. But here he was always quiet whenever I ask him if he loved you."

Georgia sighed and sagged. She had her suspicions. Georgia bet Jake put on an act in Alabama, convincing Bain he was still in love with Georgia. But here he wasn't afraid to tell the truth. And it hurt Georgia greatly.

"I love you, sweetie," Georgia whispered as she rubbed Blair's cheek with her thumb. "No matter what happens with your daddy and I... I always will. Be here for you. And love you."

"You pwomise?"

"I promise." Georgia kissed Blair's forehead. She pulled her into her lap and snuggled with her until Blair fell asleep in Georgia's arms a few minutes later.

Stephen walked over to sit next to Georgia, his arm behind her. He kissed her forehead, something he started doing to show her that he loved her. "You're so cute with her," he whispered, not wanting to wake Blair.

"Thank you," Georgia mumbled quietly.

"It reminds me of when you were that age."

Georgia sighed heavily, thinking about her mom. That was when she realized her dad was thinking about her, too. Stephen was looking out for Georgia, checking her ovaries and heart to make sure that she was okay. Georgia usually didn't take naps. She could understand her dad's scare. He thought maybe she had ovarian cancer sooner than her mom did. It was hereditary.

Georgia remembered when her mom's mom died from it. She never got to get to know the woman, only hearing stories about how amazing she was. Georgia was just a toddler when her grandma died. She remembered the feelings in the room. Looking back, she got thrown into the memory.

*There she was, again. Watching her mom as her dad comforted her. Rayleigh had her face buried in Stephen's chest as she cried. Georgia was only two years old. But she felt the raw feelings of sadness. She wanted to comfort her mom as she hid in the closet.*

*But she didn't come out. Georgia listened as Stephen comforted Rayleigh, hearing him whisper to her. He kissed her temple, rubbed her back, then gave her a tight squeeze.*

*"Ovarian cancer," Rayleigh whispered. She looked up at her husband. "Stephen. She died from ovarian cancer."*

*Stephen shook his head. "We should get you checked. Make sure you don't have it. It can be hereditary."*

*Rayleigh shivered, tears streaming down her face. "Could it be why I'm so tired suddenly?"*

*Stephen nodded his head. "It very well could be. But let's go find out."*

*Rayleigh nodded her head, letting Stephen take her hand and lead her away. Georgia waited a few minutes after the coast was clear, not wanting to get caught for eavesdropping.*

Georgia sighed and sagged. It was the start, she bet. If they caught it, now, she could live for another ten years like her mom did. Oh, Georgia hoped it wasn't too late. She felt tired and took naps for six months now. If it was too late, she'd only have a few more months to live.

*~*~*

Jake got in the cabin, ready to call Bain. But when he pulled out his phone, it didn't connect to the Wi-Fi right away. Was the power out? That's… Odd…

Jake checked the fridge. It was running. He checked a light in the living room. It was working.

Then what was going on? Jake's phone connected to the Wi-Fi earlier!

He went into the little office and checked it. The router was missing. Jake shook his head. Why was the router gone? Did someone come by and take it? Jake searched the office for it. But when he didn't find it, he was dumbfounded as to what happened between now and the time he left this morning.

Jake looked at his phone to notice it suddenly connected to the Wi-Fi. Suspicious, he looked in the small nook where electricians put an outlet for the internet. Sure enough, there it was.

"Huh," Jake dragged out, his eyebrows furrowed in confusion. He shook his head after a moment, forgetting about the move of the router. His phone started ringing, indicating Blakely was calling him. "Hey, Blakely." Jake answered. "What's up?"

"Oh, thank god you answered," Blakely breathed. She sounded relieved. "For a moment, I thought something happened. I tried calling all morning."

"What's going on?"

"I couldn't do it, Jake."

Jake stopped in the doorway of the kitchen. Suspicion settled in his gut. She couldn't… The poor thing needed to be put down!

"I couldn't kill the cute thing," she went on.

"Blakely," Jake dragged out. "It has rabies!"

"But…"

"Put it down, Blakely!" Jake insisted. "Put it out of its misery. Please!"

Blakely went quiet.

"Blakely. What's going on?"

"The cat's having a seizure," she said.

"It's going." Jake walked up the stairs to go into his bedroom. "The poor thing is in pain."

"No. Jason, wait!" Blakely yelled away from the phone. A gunshot was heard. Everything went quiet, making Jake feel better for the poor cat that suffered through rabies.

It needed to be let go. It didn't deserve to suffer.

"Jake," Blakely asked, sounding heartbroken. "I could use you right now."

Jake sighed and sagged. As much as he would love to come home… Bain was right. Blakely was with Jason. They were about to get married. Jake needed to back off and be respectful. He shook his head.

"I'm sorry, Blakely," Jake mumbled. "But I can't. I need to be here. With Blair and Georgia."

"But, Jake!"

"No but's." Jake interrupted. "I'm sorry."

Blakely sighed into the phone. "You're a good dad. I hope Georgia will see that. She deserves you."

"She doesn't deserve someone like me," Jake mumbled. "She deserves better."

"When are you going to realize that all Georgia wanted was the best for you?" Blakely asked sincerely. "She wanted to be a family. Have that same connection the two of you had in the beginning."

"Blakely, don't tell me what she wanted," Jake warned.

"As a long-lost friend, Jake… Please, don't end it with her."

"Don't you dare try to give me relationship advice. You left!"

"I didn't leave!" Blakely insisted. "Your mother did!"

"She disowned me, Blakely!" Jake snapped. "And you weren't there!"

"So, you chased after me with your new wife," she sighed. "How mature does that make you?"

"Blakely, don't do this to me." Jake warned with a growl. After all of these years. His first love was finally fighting with him.

"Bain was right," Blakely growled. "I should've moved across the waters."

"Blakely," Jake dragged out, pleading with the woman he missed so much. "Baby. Don't-."

"Don't 'baby' me, Jake. I came around on Sundays so you weren't lonely," she reminded him. "Not to fuck you! That was Georgia's job!"

Jake winced.

"I moved on, Jake!" Blakely dragged out. "I'm not in love with you. Georgia is."

"Blakely, don't end it with me," he pleaded anyway. "I beg you."

"You should've begged for me to stay when I was leaving," she said. "Not ten years later."

Tears filled Jake's eyes as he felt his heart tear. He couldn't lose her! Not now! They were best friends!

"Goodbye, Jake. I'll make sure Waldo makes it to you safely."

Jake listened as Blakely hung up. His phone beeped a couple times to initiate the end of the phone call. He put his phone down on the bed, ready to give up on life. He so wanted her back. Blakely. But she was right. He was married to Georgia.

More driven than ever to get the divorce, Jake changed his shirt before heading back out. He was going back. And he was getting Georgia's signature. Jake got in the car and started it. He backed it up, got on the road, and headed back for Franklin Basin. But when he got to Stephen's property that was above it thirty minutes later, no one was there. Where was everybody? Did they all go to Bear Lake?

Well… There was only one way to find out.

# Chapter 20

Georgia looked at her phone as she, Stephen, and Blair entered Bear Lake. Her phone went off like crazy, notification after notification. A few texts came in. A voicemail came in. Then Jake's name showed up on the screen.

Georgia sighed and sagged. She couldn't believe this! Jake just won't let his daughter be with her mom! Georgia declined the phone call, not wanting to talk to her husband. She had other things to worry about. And better things to do!

On the way to get a burger and a shake with her beloved family, Georgia wanted to enjoy this time with them. She didn't want Jake to ruin it. He tried calling again. And again. Georgia kept declining his phone call, hoping he would lose signal.

All she ever wanted was for Jake to love her. Treat her the way he treated Blakely. She'd seen the way the two of them were together. She had suspicions they were once lovers. But she didn't want to bring it up to him, in fear that they would get into an argument about it.

Georgia felt her dad's eyes on her as Jake tried calling, once again. She did her best to ignore him. But his stare burned into her skull. After a few minutes she finally caved in.

"What?" Georgia asked.

"Just answer it," Stephen replied. "And I can give him a piece of my mind."

Georgia looked at him with a glare. "There's children in the car."

"I don't give a shit," Stephen grumbled.

"Yeah, well. I do," she insisted. "We're talking about her father, here."

Stephen glanced back in the backseat before looking out the windshield. "She's asleep."

Georgia sighed in defeat. She looked at her phone as it started buzzing. Jake was trying to call once again. Georgia finally decided to answer. She put it on speaker phone and held it up between her and Stephen.

"Georgia, what the fuck?!" Jake snapped on the phone. "You know I don't like it when-,"

"Curse out my daughter, again, and I will end you," Stephen threatened with a growl, cutting Jake off.

Jake went quiet for a moment. "Stephen, this is a conversation for Georgia and I. You don't need to get involved."

"I have every right to be involved," Stephen spat. "She's my baby. My daughter."

"Yes," Jake agreed. "But-,"'

"Don't '*but*' me, Jake." Stephen interrupted. "If you don't stop harassing Georgia, I will have her put a restraining order against you. You understand me?"

Jake went quiet.

"Do you understand me?" Stephen enunciated, making himself clear.

Georgia knew that tone. Stephen was getting threateningly close to finding Jake and ending him.

"Clearly," Jake mumbled. "Can I talk to my wife, please?"

Stephen growled, unsatisfied with his conversation with the man. But he let it go. He motioned at Georgia with his chin. "Go ahead," he grumbled.

Georgia took her phone off speaker then put it to her ear. "What?"

"Where are you?" Jake pressed. "I have papers for you to sign."

"I'm not signing anything, Jake. You can forget it."

"Georgia!"

"I'm trying to have a nice day with my family," Georgia snapped, interrupting Jake. "If you don't want a part of that, that's your own damn fault. Now, let me enjoy our daughter."

"She's coming home with me, Georgia," Jake warned. "Back to Alabama."

Georgia narrowed her eyes, furrowing her eyebrows as she glared out the windshield. "You can forget it, asshole."

*"Georgia May Farr,"* Jake started, snapping at Georgia.

She hung up on him, unable to continue the conversation. She knew he would continue to try and call. Georgia decided to do the right thing. She blocked Jake's number, not wanting to hear from him for the rest of the day. She would unblock him when she was ready to talk to him again.

"Please, tell me you blocked him," Stephen mumbled, breaking the silence.

Georgia nodded her head. "Yeah," she whispered. She looked up at her dad. "Yeah, he won't be able to get a hold of me all day."

"Good."

Georgia looked down at her lap. "He won't be able to get a hold of me until I'm ready to talk to him."

Stephen rubbed Georgia's knee comfortingly. His eyes met her eyes for a moment. "I'm proud of you."

Warmth spread in Georgia's chest. It filled her and all she could think of doing was appreciate her dad. "Thanks, Dad," she whispered.

Stephen nodded his head before looking out the windshield. "I love you, sweetie. No matter what happens. You'll always be my baby girl. I never want anyone else."

"No matter what life puts us through?"

"I'll always choose you as my daughter." Stephen breathed, looking at Georgia. "You and your mother are the best things to ever happen to me. I truly love you two."

Georgia nodded her head. She scooted over to her dad to snuggle in with him, grateful to know that he loved her.


*~*~*

Georgia sat down next to Stephen with their order. He instantly reached into the bag, pulling out two French fries. Georgia stared at him in disbelief.

"How dare you?" she asked nonchalantly.

Stephen looked at her with a teasing glint in his eyes. He shoved the fries in his mouth, keeping eye contact with his daughter.

"*Jerk*." Georgia teased.

"I love you," Stephen started as Georgia pulled their burgers out of the bag. "But I get to have first dibs on the fries we share."

Georgia looked up at him just to raspberry at him. He flicked her tongue with his finger, but not hard. Georgia withdrew her tongue, knowing the message her dad was giving her. Mess around and find out. She wasn't going to push him to that point. She knew what usually happened.

Stephen would embarrass Georgia in front of everybody. And she didn't want that. Georgia gave Blair her cheeseburger after unwrapping it for her. Blair eagerly took it. She took her first bite of the burger, tears filling in her eyes.

"What's wrong, sweetie?" Georgia asked sweetly, rubbing Blair's back comfortingly.

"Daddy," Blair whispered. "He's here."

Georgia snapped her eyes up. She looked around for Jake calmly, but on the inside she was freaking out. She thought she told him to stay away! All he wanted to do was tear their family apart! What was wrong with him?!

Stephen stood up abruptly. Georgia looked up at him before following his gaze. That was when she found him. Jake was talking with a friend, laughing and smiling. Oh, Georgia hoped this was just a coincidence.

Jake knew where she went for a burger, shake, and fries with her family. But she was hoping he didn't follow her here. Stephen tried to start for Jake, but Georgia stopped him, grabbing his wrist. She felt her dad's eyes on her. She pulled him down, making him sit next to her. Georgia decided to strike up a conversation with him, putting her elbow on the table and looking at him.

"So, Dad, I was wondering," Georgia started.

"Yeah," Stephen dragged out.

"Amanda…" she teased, "from the other day."

Stephen looked at his daughter.

"Was she a girlfriend at all?"

"No," he said. "But while you and Gavin were talking, she and I decided to try and date. Give it a shot."

"Yay!" Georgia clapped her hands excitedly, eager for her dad to date someone he kind of liked. Plus, it would be cool to have a step-brother like Gavin. He may be drop dead gorgeous. But unfortunately, Georgia wouldn't be able to advance on him. He only thought of her as a friend. And she had to respect him. She didn't want to push any boundaries since she wanted a step-brother anyway.

"What are we celebrating?" A familiar voice from just a couple days ago spoke up.

Georgia looked up at Amanda, who was holding a delicious shake. "My dad just told me the good news."

"Oh," Amanda laughed. She sat down on the other side of the table with Gavin, who was holding his own shake. While Amanda's looked like it was raspberry, Gavin's looked like it was peanut butter. "I wouldn't celebrate just yet. We were just talking."

"Yeah, but. It's exciting!" Georgia gushed. "My dad needs to get back out in the dating world."

Gavin leaned forward, his eyes on Georgia. "And so does my mom." He winked at her.

Georgia blushed, wondering what Gavin was thinking. He sat up as he smiled at her, making her try to hide her blush. "Stop it, Gavin." Georgia teased. "You don't want us to be siblings."

"Actually, I could use a sister," he shrugged. "All I've got is brothers."

"And sisters-in-law," Amanda dragged out, setting her hand on Gavin's wrist. "He's got two older brothers that are married. Gavin's the youngest."

"Rayleigh and I tried for years," Stephen started. "We wanted to start at the same time all of our friends started having kids. But sadly." Stephen looked at Georgia lovingly. "We only had one amazing daughter."

"Thanks, Dad," Georgia whispered under her breath. She looked down at her burger, feeling shy suddenly. She was flattered by the compliment, but it was weird. She never got compliments from her dad before!

"Rayleigh couldn't have anymore after Georgia," Stephen went on. "Her ovaries just practically gave up trying."

"I'm so sorry, Stephen," Amanda breathed.

Georgia watched Amanda's hand sneak over and land on Stephen's wrist.

"It must've been so hard to lose her."

Georgia felt her dad's eyes on her.

"It was," Stephen spoke up. "But I'm proud to have my daughter. She looks so much like her mother."

"She does." Amanda cooed.

Georgia looked up at her and their eyes met.

"You got her face, but your eyes scream your dad," Amanda added. "You're absolutely beautiful."

"Thank you."

Gavin snorted, making Georgia give him a glare. "And I'm the prettiest of you all," he said in a high-pitched tone. He seemed to be doing better today!

Amanda smacked him with the back of her hand lightly.

"Ow!"

"Oh, that didn't hurt." Amanda looked at her son. "You, big baby," she dragged out.

"I'm sensitive," Gavin said in a teasing hurtful tone, rubbing his arm Amanda hit.

"Oh, brother," she rolled her eyes, grabbing the spoon in her shake.

"That's not what you said last night."

"Oh, don't get me started!"

Georgia and Stephen giggled, knowing the parent, child bickering way too well. They did that almost constantly!

"What'd she say last night?" Georgia asked, curious to know.

Amanda pointed at Gavin, giving him the look. "You tell her and I'm taking your phone away for a week."

Gavin gave Georgia a wry look, a small smirk on his face. "'Oh, Gavin," Gavin said in a high-pitched voice as he tried to mimic his mom. "'Stop it! You're gonna make me pee my pants!'"

Georgia burst out laughing, leaning over the table. She couldn't help but laugh! The way that was relatable anymore! After having Blair, Georgia had times where she nearly peed her pants from laughing too hard or jumping on the trampoline.

"It's a woman thing, Gavin," Stephen put in. "After they have just one child they start leaking."

Gavin giggled at Georgia as she continued laughing, unable to stop. She put her wrist to her mouth as she looked at him.

"Rayleigh had that issue," Stephen defended Amanda.

Georgia nodded her head, agreeing with her dad. She had that problem. As if Amanda knew why she was laughing, the woman laughed with her. But not as hard.

"If you ask me, though," Stephen said a little low. "It's just an excuse so you don't embarrass them."

Just like that Georgia was out of her laughing fit, looking at her father. "That is so not true," she defended herself and Amanda.

"You couldn't be further from the truth!" Amanda agreed.

Stephen looked at her. "Oh, yeah?"

"Yeah," Amanda dragged out.

Stephen shook his head. "That's not what Rayleigh said!"

Amanda raspberried at him, her tongue sticking out. Gavin instantly flicked her tongue with his finger, making her withdraw her muscled organ. Georgia snorted. That was what Stephen did to her whenever she did that to him! She put her elbow on the table and covered her smirk with her fist, all eyes on her.

"Sorry," Georgia whispered around her fist.

"Anyway," Stephen continued after a quiet moment. He looked at Gavin. "What were you doing to make her wet her britches?" He blinked his eyelids a few times at the returned missionary.

"I was making her laugh," Gavin spoke up. He cleared his throat as the speaker at the burger shop called out his name. "And uh…" He cleared the frog that seemed to be stuck in his throat. "I biffed it into the basketball pole a few times." Gavin quickly got up to go get his food.

Amanda snorted. "We were playing Horse last night."

"I haven't played that in ages!" Georgia put in as Trevor and Jessica found her and Stephen, sitting down next to Blair and saying hi to everyone. Georgia quickly said a hello.

"What game?" Trevor asked.

"Horse." Georgia looked around Jessica to see him.

"Oh my gosh," Trevor dragged out. "Last time I played was in middle school!"

"Right?" Georgia dragged out excitedly. She looked at Amanda. "Do you have a cabin around here?"

"My father does." Amanda looked at Georgia as Gavin came back with their food and sat down next to her. "If y'all wanna come play, you can. We'd love to have you."

"Georgia? Play basketball?" Jake asked on the other side of the fence.

All eyes landed on him in a glare.

"Man, if you can get her to do that," he went on anyway, "I'd love to be there."

"Jacob Farr," Amanda said. "Right?"

"Yeah," Jake dragged out. "How do you know my name?"

"Your mother."

Jake winced. "Bella?"

Amanda nodded her head. "That's right. She came to see me after the bridal shower." She looked at Georgia. "Which, by the way, I heard was absolutely beautiful."

Georgia motioned her chin at Amanda, her eyes on the blond-haired woman. "Thank you."

Amanda looked at Jake. "If you wanna play against Georgia here, be my guest."

Jake smiled as he laughed. He hung his head for a moment before finally looking at Georgia with that devil look. Shit… He was challenging her. "I would love to," he breathed.

Growls were heard from Trevor and Stephen as they protected one of their own, Georgia.

# Chapter 21

Stephen opened the door for Georgia, not ready to see Jake so soon. He'd backed off earlier during lunch. But he still decided to challenge Stephen's baby girl. He was going to whip Jake's ass if he tried anything. Stephen let his hand land on Georgia's waist, wrapping his arm around her protectively.

"Let me get my daughter," Georgia whispered.

"I'll get 'er," Stephen whispered. "She's still sleeping."

Georgia nodded her head, too worked up to think straight. Stephen could tell. At the Murk's residence in Bear Lake, Stephen almost forgot how wealthy Amanda's family was. He knew she was going to inherit everything since her brothers and sister were estranged from their father. They burnt bridges with him a long time ago. And it sounded like they never came back around. Amanda still loved her father no matter how awful he was to her. But she mostly wanted his business to continue when he was gone.

Stephen opened the back door of his truck, where Blair was fast asleep. He carefully unbuckled her seatbelt. She mewled as he gently grabbed her, but she didn't wake. Stephen held onto her as he closed the door quietly. He joined Georgia's side as they headed for the back, where the pool and basketball court were. It was quiet up at the front of the house.

But when they got to the back, Stephen caught Amanda swing dancing with Gavin to some music. They seemed to be having a good time. There were good vibes at the moment. But Stephen knew that was going to change when Jake got here. Stephen laid Blair down on the outside couch, where there were a couple of blankets. He helped her get comfortable before walking over to Amanda and intervening. She spun into him, giving him the chance to take her hand and spin her around.

"You made it!" Amanda smiled at Stephen.

His heart skipped a beat, remembering what it felt like to be free. "I wouldn't miss this for the world." As Stephen spun around with Amanda as they swing danced, she looked over at the couch Blair was sleeping on.

"Well, I'm glad you came. And with the little one!" Amanda looked up at Stephen as he brought her in. Their eyes met. "She'd be more comfortable inside."

Stephen nodded his head. "Georgia's worked up thanks to Jake. He hasn't really been that nice towards her since he's been home."

"Well, let's help her loosen up." Amanda pulled away from Stephen. She led him over to Blair, picked the little four-year-old up, then took her inside.

Stephen caught Georgia's stare, she was looking out at the lake. He acknowledged her with a lift of his chin, asking her if she was okay. She nodded her head before looking back out. She was clearly stressed. Heartbroken.

Stephen's heart reached out to his daughter, wishing he could take her pain away. He followed Amanda inside, getting thrown back to his teenage years as he walked through the house. He remembered how it used to be in here.

The couches were bigger and more comfortable, showing off the eighties style. The walls had wallpaper instead of paint. The kitchen had a retro sink and a retro fridge. Everything had changed to the fancier style and Stephen missed it.

He followed Amanda into a bedroom upstairs, one that was decorated for a little one. He looked around the room, recognizing it. This was Amanda's old room. On the right wall that was now painted yellow had a couple of floating shelves with little kid toys. It used to be bright pink with posters of rock bands Amanda loved as a kid and a teenager.

Stephen took a step inside the bedroom to look at the white dresser that used to be

Amanda's. He remembered how it once had her jewelry and makeup kits on top of it. Now, it had a teddy bear and a night light.

"Does she sleep with a night light?" Amanda asked in a whisper.

Stephen looked at her. "Georgia didn't say anything."

Amanda nodded her head. "Okay." She started for Stephen, who couldn't help but tease her.

"You know. I remember when this was your room," he mumbled. "You had the biggest crush on the lead singer of that rock band. What was their name? Banjo vibes?"

Amanda giggled, a smile on her face. "BandLo Tribe." She corrected.

"My bad."

"Let's let Blair sleep," she murmured. "We don't wanna wake her."

"You're right." Stephen took Amanda's hand and led her out of the bedroom. "Did your dad give you the house, yet?"

"We've been working on that." Amanda decided to take the lead, pulling her hand out of Stephen's.

"How's that going?" He watched her, wishing she wouldn't taunt him. But he still enjoyed her tease.

"Like it should. No trouble so far. Knock on wood." Amanda knocked on the small side table at the hall's doorway that divided it from the small living room. She turned around to look up at Stephen. "He's changed, Stephen," she whispered softly. "Ever since I decided to stick around… He's turned a little soft."

Stephen nodded his head, grateful to hear the news. "I'm happy for you, Amanda," he breathed. Truly he was. Stephen wanted Amanda to have the best in life. He always adored and admired her as a friend growing up, more interested in Rayleigh. But now that she was gone, Stephen couldn't help but wonder if he could be more than friends with Amanda. They could always try. And if it didn't work in the end… Well… Hopefully they could go back to being friends. Stephen couldn't let it go badly between him and Amanda.


*~*~*

Georgia looked out at the scenery, the lake a dark color under the night sky. It reflected the stars perfectly, showing the philosophy of a round world. It was beautiful, making Georgia wish she could escape into the world's beauty and forget everything. She didn't want to forget about Blair. But she did want to forget about Jake.

The man was inexorable. So much so, he never changed for anyone. He just did whatever he wanted. But to find out he started going to church… Was it really for Georgia? Or did Blakely convince him to go with her? Georgia sighed heavily as someone sat next to her, unable to think about Blakely and Jake together. She hated the idea.

"Ready to take him on?" Trevor asked lowly.

Georgia nodded her head. "Did you convince Russ to come?"

"Yeah," Trevor whispered. "All I had to say was Jake was coming."

Georgia nodded her head, again, grateful for such an amazing family and an amazing friend. Taelynn sat on Georgia's other side and rubbed her shoulders.

"You got this," Taelynn soothed comfortingly. "I know you'll beat him."
"Thanks, Tae."

"You're welcome," Taelynn mumbled. She continued to rub Georgia's shoulders, comforting her the best she could.

"How do you do it, Tae?" Georgia mumbled. "You have two beautiful daughters with your first baby daddy."

"He and I don't get along very well," Taelynn shrugged. "But when it comes to our girls we agree on a lot of things. Maybe it will be the same for you."

Georgia sighed heavily, defeated. "I doubt it," she mumbled. She quickly glanced at her beloved cousin. "I'm sure he'll want nothing to do with me and everything with Blair. He'll fight with me over custody. Try to say I'm not well."

Taelynn nodded her head, considering Georgia's words. "We won't let him win," she whispered.

"Thank you," Georgia whispered.

Male hands rubbed Georgia's shoulders as someone sat behind her, his legs wrapping around hers. His lips landed on her ear. "We've got to loosen you up," Russ breathed. "So, you can beat his ass."

Georgia nodded her head, grateful for such an amazing friend and amazing family. They all supported her. And they all wanted her to be happy. Clapping sounded behind Georgia, making her jump and scaring her with how loud it was.

"You're still trying, but I'm not convinced," Jake spoke up. "She only liked you as a friend growing up, Russel."

"Oh, fuck you," Russ snapped.

"You know what?" Georgia snapped softly. She stood up, turned around to face Jake, and glared at him.

Oh, he looked good. He was wearing Georgia's favorite gray button up she always wore in the mornings. How she wanted to snatch it off of Jake and steal it as of this moment. But she didn't let his good looks and muscled body get to her this time.

"I love you, Jacob Lee Farr," Georgia snapped, wanting to get a point across. "I never wanted anyone else. Yes, Russ is only a friend. But he treats me better than you ever did! Now, drop the attitude! Before I drown you in this very pool behind me!"

Jake stared at Georgia in disbelief, his jaw dropped.

"I'm in love with you! And I always will be!" She shook her head. "I may have forgotten about the life I had with you and Blair for six months, but I didn't forget my love for you! It was still there and I couldn't figure out who it was for! Now, that you're back with our daughter I now know! And if you still want Blakely after all of this…?"

"Oh," Russ drew out, sitting in front of Georgia with his knees up.

Georgia shook her head, her eyes on Jake in a glare. "Then you're messed up," she whispered.

"Let's make a bet, then," Jake started. "I win, you sign the divorce papers. You win, and I'll stay here with Blair for just a little longer."

"Deal," Georgia snarled, glaring at Jake.

It was silent between them for a while, no one speaking up. Georgia's heart pounded in her chest, reminding her why she was still alive. Blair was her everything. And she was going to win her family back no matter what it took.

"Alright," Russ finally spoke up. "Let's get this game started."

"Not without my dad," Georgia replied, keeping her glaring eyes on Jake.

"I'm right here, baby," Stephen said at the side of the house.

"Then let's do this." Georgia growled.

*~*~*

Jake was ready. He followed everyone to the basketball court, pumped to take Georgia on. He wanted that divorce, no matter what she said. He didn't love her anymore. And why should he? She had no hold on him anymore! Ready to get what he wanted he watched for the ball. Some guy bounced it to Georgia, who looked like she was going to be sick. Jake lunged forward, running towards the ball and taking it from Georgia before she could catch it.

"Jake," Georgia dragged out as she snapped. "You're such a dick!"

Jake turned around and looked at Georgia challengingly. "You were too slow."

She leaned forward, letting him see the top of her breasts. "Then shoot." She ordered, distracting him with her cleavage.

He didn't think she still had that effect on him. But apparently, she did. Jake shook his head to clear it then took his shot. He threw the basketball towards the hoop, but it bounced off the rim and into Georgia's hands.

"Ha," she scoffed. "My turn."

Jake nodded his head. "Okay," he dragged out. "Go for it," he breathed seductively.

Georgia glared at him before taking her shot, throwing the basketball a few feet away from the hoop. The net swished as the ball made it through. That was a lucky shot.

Everybody joined in on the game of Horse. Avery joined with Ashton after two people got the first letter, Russ and Trevor's wife Jessica. One was pregnant, though, having every reason to miss whenever the baby kicked or she had a moment of discomfort.

Jake was able to clear his head from Georgia's spell when she first cast it on him by showing off her cleavage, making it into the hoop every time. She always made it after him, showing off by standing a foot behind the spot she's supposed to shoot from.

Russ was the first one out. Then it was Avery. Stephen always high fived his girlfriend whenever one of them made it. But his girlfriend was the next one out. What was her name, again?

Amanda? Her son did very well, showing off his height and skill. He must be a professional, making it every time.

"Hey, Gavin," Georgia called out to him as he had the ball.

Gavin looked over at her. She lifted her shirt to show off her bra covered breasts.

It got a growl out of Jake, making him territorial of his wife. She was getting to him and he hated it. But he had to admit she was being fun, again. He couldn't resist what he wanted to do to her. But he did his best to keep from walking across the basketball court and kissing her. His head told him it wasn't worth saving his marriage. But his heart told him a different story.

Gavin took his shot, distracted by Georgia's breasts. He missed, getting an H. It was finally Jake's turn, again. Distracted, he took his shot, unable to stay focused. He missed. With Georgia's shot, she got the ball swishing in the hoop from the side.

Stephen took his turn, but it seemed he was distracted. He missed, getting the last letter in

Horse. He was out. A second ball finally came in and Jake looked over to see it came from Amanda.

"Double the fun," Amanda put in. "Same rules."

Jake nodded his head, trying to clear it from his wife's distractions. But he was starting to fail. What was wrong with him? He couldn't love her! Not after she ran! She was at fault for all of this!

Jake got a ball after Trevor and Russ took their shots and missed. Gavin stood in a spot as Jake took the opposite side. They both threw at the same time. The basketballs clashed together, bouncing off from one another and going opposite directions.

One of them hit Georgia straight in the stomach, where her ovaries were, making her double over in pain. She screamed out loudly as if she was in agony.

"Stephen," Avery asked in uncertainty. "Does she…?" She trailed off, unable to finish her sentence. She looked horrified.

Jake watched the scene, confused as to what was going on. Stephen was at Georgia's side, holding her hand as she clung onto his. He muttered in her ear before nodding his head to Avery, confirming an unspoken question.

"Russ," Avery dragged out. She turned around to look at Russ. "It's true."

"*No,*" Russ said, his voice rocky.

"Trevor," Stephen spoke up. "I need you to take her to the emergency room. Now!"

"He can't," Jessica said.

Stephen looked at her and realization hit his face. Jake looked over to see Jessica's water broke, her pants a few shades darker than they should be. In the chaos, her water had broken.

"Come on, baby," Stephen whispered. "Let's get you in the truck."

"No, don't," Georgia mewled in pain as Stephen tried to pick her up. "It hurts."

"We need to get you to the hospital, Georgie," he cooed. "Fast. A cyst might have burst."

That's when it finally hit Jake. Ovarian cancer. Rayleigh had it. It only made sense that Georgia had it. No… It was too soon!

"I'll take her," Jake spoke up. All eyes were on him. "Stephen, let me take her. Please. You go get our daughter."

Silence fell upon everyone as they held their breath.

"Fine," Stephen grumbled, glaring at his son-in-law.

# Chapter 22

Georgia waited patiently, even though her arms were wrapped around her stomach as pain surged through her gut. She hurt greatly. She couldn't think straight. So much pain… And for what? Ovarian cancer? Dear Lord…

Georgia hoped it was just PCOS, a disease that copied ovarian cancer with cysts. She couldn't bear the thought of leaving her daughter anytime soon. Jake stood next to her, his hand stroking her hair comfortingly. This was a first for him since they got married!

"I'm here," Stephen whispered next to Georgia. He wrapped his arm around her. "Blair is with Amanda. She said she'd be fine there."

Georgia nodded her head, sniffling. Tears kept coming. She was in so much pain, she couldn't stop crying. Gosh, it hurt! Why did it have to hurt so much?! It wasn't like she was dying! …Or was she?

Georgia panicked on the inside, wanting to give her daughter more time with her. She couldn't! Could a cyst popping on her ovaries cut back her time with her family? Georgia could hardly pay attention to her surroundings. So, when she finally noticed the doctor in the room, she wondered how long he'd been there.

"Any good news at all?" Stephen pressed.

The doctor shook his head. "I'm so sorry, Stephen. But she has less time than Rayleigh by not even half."

"How is this possible?" Stephen breathed.

"The cyst that popped spread infection in her ovaries," the doctor explained. "Who knows what could've happened if you didn't bring her in, in time."

"It was Jake." Stephen looked over at Georgia's husband, who seemed rigid next to her for some reason. What was he thinking? "He brought her in."

The doctor looked at Jake. "Do you have any relation to Miss Rhinehart, Jacob?"

"It's Mrs. Farr," Jake corrected the doctor. "She's my wife."

The doctor nodded his head. "Well, if she doesn't have one, she should fill out a will while she can." The doctor walked over to Georgia and held out his hand to her, showing off two pills. "For the pain."

Georgia nodded her head, grateful for relief. She quickly took the pills and popped them into her mouth. The doctor handed her a glass of water. She gladly took it, taking a big long drink and finishing the cup.

"Georgie," Stephen breathed, sounding heartbroken.

She was able to clear her head after a moment. The pain pills started to work quickly but the doctor handed her another set of pills. That was when she recognized him. Her mom's doctor. The one that diagnosed Rayleigh with ovarian cancer.

No…

"I'm sorry, Georgie," Doctor Garrison whispered, his eyes filled with sorrow. "But you have stage four cancer."

Georgia shook her head, tears filling her eyes. *No!* She couldn't! This couldn't be happening!

"How long do I have?" Barely audible to the human ear, Georgia wondered if Doctor Garrison caught her words.

He offered her the pills. "This is for the infection."

"But will they matter?"

"They'll slow the infection down and give you a little more time with your family," he explained.

She knew what he was doing. Doctor Garrison was stalling.

"How long do I have?" She pressed. She was stern, wanting answers.

"Six months," Doctor Garrison finally replied. "A whole year if you stay on top of your medicine."

A year would have to do. But Georgia wanted much longer. She wanted to watch her baby grow up!

"Georgie," Jake finally spoke up, sounding frantic. He got in front of her and held onto her upper arms, his blue eyes searching her brown eyes. "Hey," he whispered. "I'm not going anywhere. Okay?"

Georgia searched Jake's eyes, trying to figure out what he was saying.

"I'm with you," he promised. "All the way. I'm never letting you go."

"Jake," she whispered, "what are you saying?"

"Consider the papers thrown away," he said. "I love you, Georgie." He shook his head. "And I don't wanna lose our family."

Blair… She'd done this. She'd convinced Jake somehow.

But after all of this time… Did Georgia want to take the man back? She wouldn't be here if it wasn't for him! She shook her head at him, unsure if she could forgive him for bursting one of her cysts on her ovaries. He brushed her bangs back and tucked them behind her ear.

"I'm not leaving, Georgia," Jake mumbled, love filled in his eyes. "I'm here to stay."

Tears filled Georgia's eyes as she started to catch on. But she knew what she had to do.

# About the Author

BreAnn Hanks is a small-town author and country-blues singer, currently living with her mom and step-dad since she's always had a job so close to home.

Hanks is an animal lover, having a dog and two cats at the moment. But if she could, she would start a sanctuary for rescue animals or be an animal foster.

Hanks decided to do something different, writing not just fantasy romance, but romance as well. Sweet Georgia is her first attempt at a family-oriented romance, where the main character has challenges of her own.

If you can't wait to find out more about Hanks, head over to her website, where she has merchandise, news, and more!

https://www.breannhanks.com

Can't wait for Sweet Avery?

Read an excerpt on the next page!

# Prologue

Jake kissed her. His wife. He kissed her for the very first time since her accident six months ago. He couldn't help himself. Finding that she had stage four ovarian cancer made him realize how precious she was. Their daughter's time with her was limited. And his time to make it up to her… Was close to none. But he could still try.

A growl came from her father next to them as he held onto what was left. He didn't care that her father was protective of her. She was his wife. And he wasn't letting her go anytime soon. He'll always be making up for what he did. Even when she was gone. But at least he could say he tried. She held onto his wrists, making him hope that they could start over. But she pushed him off of her.

"Jake, what are you doing," Georgia whispered.

Jake shook his head. "Taking you back," he mumbled.

"Not happening," Stephen growled next to Jake.

"Threaten me all you want," Jake snapped low as he turned his attention to the protective father. "Stephen. But Georgia's my wife."

"Just moments ago, you could care less of what happened to her," Stephen defended himself, his voice threateningly low. "Now, that she's got cancer you care?!" He shook his head at the younger man. "I'm not letting you ruin the rest of what she's got!"

"Dad," Georgia started, her voice shaking.

Stephen looked at her with pleading eyes. She nodded her head to him reassuringly. Jake felt her eyes on him. His blue eyes met her brown eyes.

"We'll make it work," Georgia mumbled. "For Blair. But not as husband and wife."

Jake's heart tore in his chest and it was screaming for him to run as he gaped at his beloved wife.

# Chapter 1

Avery stared at the casket, unwilling to do this. Her best friend was already planning her own funeral. And it was devastatingly heart-wrenching.

Avery looked at Georgia as she joined her side. She took her hand in hers, unwilling to go through with this.

"Please, don't do this," Avery whispered pleadingly. "I can't lose you."

Georgia looked at her best friend. "I have to," she mumbled. "There's no cure."

"But what if there was," Avery said as she turned towards her beloved friend that was like a sister to her. "What if we could find a doctor that knew a cure?"

Georgia shook her head. "Doctor Garrison is the best of the best, Avery. I'm sorry. But my death is coming whether we like it or not."

Avery sighed with a shudder, tears in her eyes.

"Marco," Russ called, his voice muffled.

Georgia sighed and sagged. "And then there's idiots like Russ, who have to pull such a sick joke."

Avery snorted and pressed her lips together, holding back a laugh. "You have to admit it lightens the mood."

"That's what he's good for," Georgia mumbled. She took a noticeable breath. "Polo!" She called.

"Marco," Russ called, again.

Avery looked at the closed casket in front of her, realizing Russ was right in front of them. She raised an eyebrow. Georgia found the pin that unlocked the casket and pulled it. She then threw the casket open.

"Polo," she yelled in Russ's face, scaring him.

He screamed and kicked his legs, jumping almost a foot. Avery laughed as he jumped out of the casket and started to pace. She couldn't help it! It was hilarious to see him get scared shitless for once!

Russ looked at Georgia as he turned towards her, pacing. He turned around to pace the other direction. You could tell by the look on his face he wasn't expecting Georgia to scare him like that. She was pretty quiet about it!

Russ turned towards his best friend, again, and pointed at her. "Don't do that, again," he warned.

Georgia giggled, a smile on her face. "You deserved it, handsome." She winked at him.

Avery wiped the tear from her laughter off her face before she came to, getting a glare from Russ. She cleared her throat and looked down, unable to look him in the face after the show he gave her for her bachelorette party last week.

Her wedding was coming up fast. And who knew how much she'd be able to enjoy when she knew her best friend didn't have much time. All

she could do was make the most of it… But it was
going to be hard. It was never easy to say goodbye
to those you loved.